Praise for Viol‹
& Scarstr

"The most romantic novel of love, marriage, sodomy, and cigarette burns of all time."
—Nick Mamatas, author of *The People's Republic of Everything*

"The hype does not disappoint."   —*The Big Smoke*

"A crushing journey into the beauty and horror of nostalgia."   —*LitReactor*

"LeVoit deconstructs Hollywood, art, and nostalgia . . . packed with crackling dialogue that rivals anything Elmore Leonard ever wrote . . . as anarchic as it is brilliant."
    —Gabino Iglesias, author of *Coyote Songs* and *Zero Saints*

"For lovers of edgy, intelligent noir."   —*The Monitor*

"LeVoit's work exists at the center of a glowing nexus where fever dream punk rock poetry collides with raw emotion and vertiginous talent. It's fucked-up, frightening, frequently funny in ways that make you feel guilty for laughing, and highly recommended."
    —Jeremy Robert Johnson, author of *Skullcrack City*

Also by Violet LeVoit

I Miss The World
Hotel Butterfly

First King Shot Press edition

King Shot Press
P.O. Box 80601
Portland, OR 97280

Cover design © 2019 Matthew Revert
www.matthewrevert.com
Typeset by Michael Kazepis

ISBN 13: 978-1-7321240-3-5
ISBN 10: 1-7321240-3-5
ASIN: B07MT4S8Y7

Printed in the United States of America and worldwide

SCARSTRUCK

VIOLET LeVOIT

KING SHOT PRESS
Portland | Athens

Every naked back at the party streaked with blood red light, *not my crowd*, the man thought, *I should go*, but before he could the lean keen teen sensation surfaced from the flesh pile and locked astonished eyes on him *oh shit, you too?* And they laughed about how they did not look like their posters and he reached out to touch him, dove for his fly, laughing mouth warm and soft *I hear stories about you, my blood brother: mark me up*, the contented sigh of a crushed-out cigarette, *this is where dreams come true—*

The crack of a breaking door. *LAPD! 288a! Put your clothes on—*

The kid grabbed at him, terror cramping his perfect features. *Save me.* Instead the man shoved him aside, scrambled out the window, ran until he tasted blood, to the car, drove fast, fast, fast . . . *did they see my face? my million dollar face?*

1

Los Angeles, 1957

The ice in his drink was cold and the sky was California blue, same color as the pool poured into the plane of concrete like a runway of glass. Ron touched the drink to his lips and didn't taste the bourbon. He could feel it, though. Fifth one of the day. Not even noon. Wind swayed the palms overhead and flicked the corners of the *Variety* half-clutched in this hand. The headlines screamed five bourbons worth of bad news. RON DASH IN GAY FLAP. Oh dear.

A figure-eight blonde came down to the pool in a coral-red swimsuit and heart-shaped sunglasses, espadrille wedges tied with pink bows around her shapely ankles, towel over her arm like a mink wrap. She scanned the patio for appreciative eyes. Ron shrank down in his deck chair and ducked behind the paper. He watched the fleshy hill of her shoulders twitch. *That's what you get for wearing a bathing suit the one February day LA is cold,* he thought.

No agents at the pool today. No talent scouts looking to anoint a new starlet. Just a shivering blonde, and an actor in a sharp suit, walking dead. He could taste the seconds ticking by.

Hollywood ran lavender, no doubt about it, but it was all a matter of who you paid to keep your secrets. Maybe *Salacious* and *Nosy* and *Do Tell* didn't tip the studio off in time. *Extra! Extra! What square-jawed "man's man" got an earful from LAPD when they busted up a kinky fag soiree in Hollywood Hills?* Tip off, my ass. They wanted that big juicy cover story all for themselves. *"He's worse than an animal," sobbed what teen heartthrob as cops took snaps of his cigarette burns?* Maybe those lace hanky phonies in upper brass didn't feel like hauling his fat out of the fire this time. Not when it's February and the beach party movies have to be in the drive-ins by June. *That little fucker should have told me I had to leave his chest alone for close-ups,* he thought. *All it takes is the secret word.*

He figured he had twenty-four hours to cash it all in. Down a last drink, sign off a hotel bill he'd never be able to pay, careen in his leased Cadillac back to Holmby Hills and shut the door. Scratch that. News travels fast in this town. Maybe it was already over. He took another sip and discovered his drink was empty.

The blonde lay back in her deck chair and tried to pretend she was basking in the heat. Her lips twitched and her goosepimply thighs shuddered. *They like to pretend I'm the only one whose dick gets hard from watching pretty things squirm. People like to suffer in this town,* thought Ron as he slid off his chair and weaved back to the hotel lobby. *The only thing that matters is who's dishing it out.*

There was a light at the end of the hotel corridor, but he wasn't going that far. "Key, please," he mumbled to the gray-haired stork of a concierge. It clattered to the desktop. Yesterday the old man had placed it in his hand.

Ron twisted out a smile. "You must read the best publications," he said.

The gray-green wallpaper swam like seaweed as he waited for the elevator. The deep blue carpet was soft beneath his loafers. Like freshly dug dirt. *Like around a grave,* he thought, and then the elevator door opened.

Ding.

The elevator Mexican wore white, and white gloves, and a pillbox hat, like an organ grinder's monkey. He wore clear skin and bright eyelashes and the kiss of youth. You could put out a cigarette in his dimples. *Ashtrays of the face,* thought Ron.

"Ninth floor," he said. The boy nodded.

Ron stood a little bit behind him as they rode.

"Haven't seen an elevator boy since I was a kid," said Ron. "I thought they were all girls and Negros nowadays."

"Guess not," shrugged the boy. His narrow shoulders twitched under his jacket.

"How old are you?"

"Nineteen." Consonants soft with *español.*

"You in pictures?"

The boy turned around. Sweet, self-conscious smile of crooked wetback teeth.

"Everyone asks me that," he replied. "But you are, right?"

Ron coughed. "Used to be. Now I'm just here."

The boy turned back to the elevator controller. "I couldn't be in movies like you," he said. "I'm too short."

"All movie stars are short." Ron reached into his breast pocket. "All of them have bad skin, bad eyes, bad breath." He extracted a cigarette from the pack. The boy fumbled in his own pocket and palmed a book of matches. It took him a few strokes to flick the head into a snarl of gunpowder. Ron leaned forward into the boy's cupped hand. "The camera makes them beautiful." He squinted into the boy's eyes and took a drag. He exhaled and the boy stifled a cough.

Ding.

"Your floor, sir." the boy said.

Ron picked a thread of tobacco from his tongue. He took in the discreet nose, the high cheekbones, the narrow jaw unmarred with stubble.

"You don't read the papers, do you?"

A little twitch of the lips. "Sometimes."

"Did you read them today?"

He saw the Adam's apple in the boy's throat bob for a moment. The swallow of someone buying time.

"So you know who I am," said Ron. He took a step closer and the boy's long dark lashes fluttered like startled butterflies. "And . . . you know *what* I am."

The boy nodded slowly. Ice-blue eyes. Bluer than California pools. *Don't see that on a Mexican every day,* Ron thought. He put the cigarette back in his mouth.

"And you still didn't mind sharing an elevator with me," he murmured, the words jouncing the cigarette between his lips.

"Sharing an elevator with you was the highlight of my day, sir." The words tumbled out, too quick and too eager, and he knew it. The boy flushed and bit his lower lip.

Ron knew now. This wasn't starstruck. Starstruck was *gee whiz* and *looky here* and *Ma, take a Kodak*. He could see it in eyes gone suddenly wide as they flapped fanning pages of autograph books in his face. *You are everything I am lacking*, starstruck said. *I never knew the name for the grey dead hole inside me but I know you have the cure.* They shoved pens at him and snatched the scribbled pages away. *My life is small and dull and I am so full of self-hate it can turn inside out like a skinned cat and destroy you.* One bobbysoxer thrust a pencil at his hands so quickly she stabbed a wasp stinger of broken graphite right into his skin. *I want a picture. I want a kiss. I want to tear off a piece of you and clutch it in my bloody fist forever.*

This boy stood, shoulders hunched like a cowed hound dog in his white jacket. A living, breathing surrender flag. *Tear off a piece of me*, his posture screamed.

Ron took a step forward. The boy inhaled sharply.

"Take off that stupid hat," said Ron.

The boy snatched it off his head and ran his fingers through his Brylcreemed bangs.

"What's your name?"

"Flaco." Softly, spoken down to the carpet. "I don't like it."

"Well, this is Hollywood," said Ron. He turned the key in the lock. "You can be whoever you want to be." He put his hand on the boy's chest, one meaty palm square on his sternum. "And you can start being him right now."

He gave the boy a shove through the open door. The boy stumbled to keep his footing and the edge of the mattress kicked into the back of his knees. He sat down hard.

"You read the article?" said Ron.

"Yeah," said the boy, half-breathless.

Ron raised his hand and struck. *Smack!* against the boy's cheek like a whipcrack of thunder. The boy's head snapped to the left. The long *café con leche* underbelly of his neck stretched out for one languid moment. The print of Ron's hand welled strawberry on his cheek.

Ron clenched his tingling palm and waited. *This is where they chicken out*, he thought. *They raise their hand to their cheek, to touch what they can't quite believe. They get their coat and well-I-never and trundle out the door.*

This boy's hands stayed at his sides. Mouth open, chest heaving. Fingers clawing the bedspread like a cat in heat.

Ron grabbed him by the hair and yanked his head back.

"You know what you're in for?" he hissed.

"I read the article," the boy gulped. His throat was dry and the lump tenting his pants was hard.

"They print lies," said Ron. He leaned in close enough to kiss. "Lies sell magazines. Lies let housewives cluck their tongues over how sick we are."

"I hope they're not lies," breathed the boy. His mouth parted like a peach torn in half and Ron took the bait. He crushed his mouth over girl-sweet lips and tasted coconut sun lotion and toothpaste and virginity in the slippery twitch of his startled tongue. The unspoiled taste made him greedy. When the boy tried to come up for air Ron bit hard on his bottom lip instead. A little yelp escaped the boy's throat and smothered into a moan. The wet nail tang of blood salted his kiss.

"Take it off," said Ron, and didn't wait for the boy's slender fingers to rise to the task. He shoved his own thick fingers in the collar of the boy's uniform and yanked down hard. *Pop, pop, pop.* Threads snapped, brass buttons hiccupped onto the floor like jumping beans. Ron parted linen to reveal a ribbed white undershirt barely hiding bird-fragile collarbones and the Salinas-flat plane of a still-teenage chest. The boy reached for his own waistband but Ron chucked him under the chin with one strangling hand and shoved him horizontal. The boy gasped tightly and it gave Ron a not-small thrill to see his slim tan fingers clutch at the ham hock of his own hairy wrist.

"Don't fight," Ron hissed into the boy's neck. *This is the city of angels*, he thought as he ripped the flimsy cotton off the boy's chest. 50 *centavos* nipples, dark as coffee. *Unspoiled and sunkissed.* He shoved his hand down the front of the boy's pants and didn't fish long for the hot stalk straining against rough cotton briefs. Slick at the tip already. *Where the sun is bright and shiny like a new copper penny.* The boy shuddered and his cock jumped hot and eager in Ron's hand. He flipped the boy onto his hollow stomach and pinned him to the bed. *And the streets are paved with dreams.* The lamp was nearby, a Beaux Arts dinosaur. He swatted it to the ground and the black enamel shattered like a bomb. He ripped the clothbound wire from the ceramic shards and wound it tightly against the boy's slim wrists, up and around the bedpost in a skin-cutting figure eight topped with a perfect knot. That merit badge was good for something.

"*Por favor* . . ." the boy said, ecstatic submission letting loose his mother tongue. His face was crushed between pillow and headboard and his hands were folded in supplication, the tourniquet wire swelling his hands. Ron pondered his meaning. *Please spare me. Please finish me. Please push me to the dark place I want to be.*

He shoved the boy's waistband down to the backs of his tight and hairless thighs. The boy's ass had a perfect Dusenberg swerve, a streamlined nobility that mocked the sharp boomerangs and Googie swoops of the Sunset Strip skyline outside. Ron traced one fingernail down the boy's spine, from the charming bump at the back of his neck, down past the muscled ribs shimmering beneath thin skin, to the spot above the crack of his ass where two shallow moon divots stared like Orphan Annie's eyes. Ron smirked. *This one's just covered in ashtrays*, he thought.

The cigarette still glowed between his lips. *Burn him*, it said in a silvery whisper only he could hear. *Ruin what's perfect. Brand him like cattle.* Ron took the cigarette between his fingers like a man aiming a dart. He looked at the boy's naked back. He thought about that other boy, that supercilious prick with the pimple cream complexion and the *Teen Jive* eyes, the one who pointed his little sissy finger right at Ron when the boys in blue arrived. That shitbag twink deserved every stupid lie he'd have to spin for every makeup girl assigned to spackle over his burns with greasepaint before the cameras rolled. This boy, this strip of caramel stretched long on rumpled white sheets, breathing hard, back shivering, bound hands locked unconsciously in prayer—he didn't deserve that. No matter how much Ron wanted it.

People get off the bus in Hollywood every day, thought Ron as he peeled off his shirt. *They smell the dead scent of Valentino and Harlow and follow their nose all the way to the great garbage heap at the bottom of this town.* The fiery erection in his own pants was nudging through the slit of his boxers. He unzipped, placed the tip of his cock against the crack of the boy's ass. He ran his hands through the boy's hair. Slick with Brylcreem. Slide it up and down that shaft. Not too greasy. It'll have to do.

"First time?" he hissed into the perfect seashell of the boy's ear.

"Everything," the boy whined, and it took a moment for Ron to realize he meant *first time for everything.*

"It'll hurt."

"Yes," breathed the boy, and that was all he needed.

He nudged the tip of his cock against the tight pucker of the boy's ass. The air hissed between the boy's teeth and his shoulders jumped and he gulped *ay dios mío, dios mío* into the bed and Ron grabbed him by the hips. One hand on the small of the boy's back, thumb spreading the cheeks. One hand gripped to his cock. The rosebud wouldn't budge. Ron spat. The boy gasped, one sharp cry, thin and shocked. The sound a virgin makes when he breaks. Dark and swallowing, opening up.

17

Orange farmers came to California, thought Ron. His hips began to pump. *They took one look at virgin soil and endless sunshine and plowed it back and forth,* back and forth, *here is life and love and light and youth* and the spray of citrus crashed into his brain and the boy howled and gulped and Ron shoved him up the bed closer closer until *bonk* the boy hit his face on the headboard and Ron almost had to laugh but the boy's ass convulsed around his dick in unfunny delight and he lost it. *Unnggh.*

The room's light got cold after orgasm. The boy panted into the mattress, hands still bound. Lukewarm nausea rose in Ron's throat. *They look good trussed when I start*, he thought. *When I'm done I feel sorry for them.* Something that needed to drown in another bourbon started to surface inside him.

He took the boy under the armpits, gently, and worried the rubbery wire loose from his wrists as he lifted him. "Come on up, kid."

The boy lifted his head. Nosebleed. Red Rorschach spattered into the pillowcase, gory butterfly under the nose. Ron went white.

"Oh, Jesus."

"It's okay." The boy sniffled and rubbed his face on his shoulder. "I don't mind." The once-perfect slope of his nose had an ugly hump. The purple was already pooling under his eyes.

"Oh, Jesus," Ron said again. "Let's take care of you."

2

They sat in the booth at Don Skinny's on Sunset, in the back where Butch the fry cook wouldn't give him hell for drinking coffee with another man. Ron smoked and the boy had a pecan roll. The top of the table was littered with shredded napkins spotted with red, like bloody tumbleweed.

"I'll get a raw steak for that eye." Ron waved for the waiter.

"I don't need it," the boy said. "Honest, I don't."

Ron nudged his own nose with his thumb and pushed a tumbler of ice water towards him. "You should see a doctor," he said. "It'll set crooked otherwise."

"I know. I like it." The boy wiped his nose again and gave a small, sheepish smile, not looking Ron in the eye. He blushed. "It's better than an autograph."

A small shiver went up Ron's spine. *A starfucker. Why didn't I see it? Unless . . .* His eyes scanned the room. The oldest trick in the book: corner a horny queer with a boy hustler and milk the secret for cash until the udder cracks and bleeds. His eyes scanned the room for the blackmail man in tow. A man sitting at the lunch counter, face hidden by the crowd, hat still on his head. The kind of person who needs to eat and run. The hat shifted and Ron caught his breath. *Darkroom Louie.* Paparazzi scum. His gut froze.

The boy nodded softly at the cigarette growing ashy and neglected in Ron's frozen hand. "You could have burned me," he said, almost a whisper. "I wouldn't mind."

Something about those words snapped Ron back to life. He fumbled in his jacket pocket as if searching for a life vest. Calfskin wallet, a fan of crisp green. The boy's blue eyes grew big as marbles.

"I don't know how much he's paying you," said Ron, waving the bills. He folded the wad in half and slid it over the table. "But you're going to take it," he said. "And you're going to leave me alone."

The boy didn't take it. He stared at the wad uncomprehendingly, as if Ron had slid him a dead mouse. "But I don't—" he started, and then looked at the wad again, something crestfallen creeping into his face.

Ron looked up. Butch the fry cook was staring at him. Ugly Popeye mug, eyes slitty with disgust. He looked ready to spit on the grill. Time to go.

Ron plucked another dollar from his pocket. "That's for the pecan roll." He slid out of the booth. "Don't follow me," he said, and didn't look back.

He almost made it out the door before one sharp finger jabbed him in the shoulder. He wheeled around.

"Hiya, pal." Darkroom Louie took a sip of coffee and raised the dark accordion of his Speed Graphic camera hanging around his neck. "Took two snaps of you and Juanita having kaffeeklatsch back there. *Movie Star News*'ll buy them. But I hear you're in the soup these days." He flicked his head to the shards of crumb on his empty pie plate. "Pay my tab?"

Ron slapped a $20 on the counter and glared at him.

Louie stared at the cash and whistled low. "That's a 35 cent tab, pal," he smiled. "My waitress is going to love you." He slid the bill over the counter.

"Let's see it," growled Ron.

Louie unlatched a switch on the camera and swung open the back. One grey lozenge of ruined film in the gate, like a little movie screen. He twirled a dial and scrolled out another portion of erased evidence before snapping the camera shut.

"How do I know there aren't more?"

"If there are, you know where I live." Louie smiled. "Come on over and break my jaw anytime."

"Don't wait for a house call," said Ron stiffly. "You'll get yours the next time I see you."

The waitress brought back Louie's tab, balanced with a little layer cake of rumpled ones. Louie cut the deck and slid half the bills back to the astonished waitress. He tucked the rest of Ron's money into his pocket and grinned.

"Don't you have to pay your business partner?" said Ron.

Louie shrugged. "Ain't nobody here but us chickens."

Ron turned. "Then what about—" He looked at the booth in the back. The boy was gone. The napkins were there, the half-eaten pecan roll slumped in a sticky lump on its plate. The money was still on the table.

Ron wheeled around. "Where is he?"

Louie put his coffee cup down. "Sorry, pal. That's a page from your date book, not mine. Oh, by the way—" He slid off the stool and tipped the brim of his hat to Ron. "Word on the street is your agent's looking for you." He pushed the front door open. Chimes and street noise swirled around his parting words. "Says he's got a meeting that can't wait."

3

"You're carrion," said Rockwell. "Both of you."

Ron sat in a deep leather club chair and watched his agent pace his office. It wasn't a big office, but Rockwell took small steps. The carpet was a touch too mauve and the faux-Greco bas reliefs on the wall looked like young girls cavorting, if you squinted.

"I don't care if that little prick Grayson is carrion," said Ron. "But I'd like to save my own neck, if I still can."

"You can." Rockwell sat down at the edge of his desk. His bowtie matched the blotter. "And that little prick is my client, too." He gestured at the beach party posters festooning the far wall of his office. *Cabana Canasta. Bikini Meanie. Who's Afraid Of the Big Bad Surf?* The tan V of Grayson Todd, shimmying in Bermuda shorts with a bevy of starlets in not-too-low-cut bikinis. Wholesome as a glass of milk. "You were young, dumb and full of cum once, too."

"Then I know how he'll be doing penance." Ron stood up and strolled to the cocktail bar beneath the window. He thought he saw his reflection in the glass before he realized it was a billboard high above The Strip. His face, leaner and handsomer than in life, clutched to some actress's cheek. "Forgot that was coming out in March," he mused as he put his drink to his lips.

"If you're lucky. Ultimate's pulling *Magnificent Fury* while you're on suspension. They'll pull *Hammer Of Fate*, too, if the fix doesn't work." He wiped his impeccable palms clean. "We're throwing them a bone."

"Who?"

"The tattle rags. Dale DeVance."

Ron winced. "He's a nice kid."

"He's a car thief. Louisiana's got a rap on him and his bootlegger family a mile long. Plus I hear his mom's an octoroon. It's the easiest kill I've got." Rockwell sighed, the sigh of a butcher who hated lambing season. "We plant a story in Malva Harper's column. The gossip mags will start sniffing. We sue for libel on the surface and feed them this underneath. It'll all be fish wrappings in a month."

Ron shook his head. "It just doesn't seem like enough."

"It's not." Rockwell leaned forward. "That's why you're doing penance, too."

Ron swallowed hard. The casting couch was one thing when he was young and hungry. But Rockwell had been his agent for years. It almost seemed like incest now.

"Don't see how one more blow job will make this all go away, Rock." His voice quavered in spite of himself.

There was a scream somewhere in the building. Maybe a woman. Too crazed for that. An animal, a wounded panther trapped between ceiling and floor. Ron jumped. Rockwell did not.

"Come take a look," he said.

They strode out into the hall, a jangling ring of keys appearing in Rockwell's hand. The screams got louder and closer. The keys opened a door, the door led to a room. Rockwell's gymnasium. Padded floor, punching bag, two way mirror along one side. Ron knew it well. They stood on the secret side of the mirror, watched three beefy men in white coats wrangle a tangle-haired blonde in a straitjacket. One shoe on, one shoe off. She kicked one man in the head high enough to pop loose the garter on her thigh. Her screams could etch glass.

"You know Lana?" said Rockwell.

Ron pressed his fingers to the glass. *Can't be*, he thought. *Lana Arleaux. Rising Star of 1953. That's what Photoplay said. I remember reading the article. I remember thinking she was pretty. She was clever. She was smarter than all of this.*

"Diddley and Cray Agency called me," said Rockwell. He didn't take his eyes off the shifting knot of angry girl and three big men. "Seems she didn't turn up for a TV bit. Three days later they pulled her out of a drunk tank in Tijuana. Not a first, apparently." He smiled. "She's very colorful. I think you'll like her."

"How much do I have to like her?"

"You're going to marry her."

Ron stepped back as if the glass was electrified. "Stop," he said.

Rockwell turned from the window. He looked Ron full in the eye, gravely. "Marriage is good cover, Ron. And good press. There's none better." He watched Lana kick and scratch at the men holding her down. "She's just a little excited right now. She's had a sedative. Give it a moment to kick in."

Ron looked through the glass. "What does she think about this . . . plan?"

"Her agent's in favor of it. Therefore, she is." He shut the door. The screams continued through the wall.

Ron winced. "And the same line of reasoning applies to me?"

Rockwell hesitated. He clapped his hand on Ron's shoulder. "I'm not a miracle worker, Ron. When Bruce Payton and Tate McCraw spent more time in their trailer than on the set of *Red Cavallo*, I buried it. Because I could." He pointed at him. "Because they made my job easy."

"I'm sure they did," snorted Ron. Bruce Payton had the tight blond curls of a Botticelli cherub and Tate McCraw could plant corn in his abdominal furrows. "And I know just what you buried. And where."

Rockwell stepped closer. His eyes narrowed. "I am a connoisseur of antique furniture, vintage wine, and unspoiled beauty—and I make no bones about my wholesome tastes. But I can't for the life of me think why a rational man would prefer cigarette burns and sailor knots to a normal act of love." His eyes narrowed. "I can bury sissy, Ron," he said, his words tight with meaning. "I can't bury *sick*. So quit holing up at Montserrat's poolside bar and face the mess you've made for yourself—like a real man would."

The drink wore off in Ron's head like theater lights gone black. He swallowed, suddenly thirsty, and turned on his heel.

"Where are you going?" said Rockwell.

"Home. Alone," he said. "To think."

"Don't think so," said Rockwell. Another scream tore through the thin wall. He smiled wanly. "You've got a date tonight."

4

He went home anyway. He took the bottle from the bar and lay down on the couch and watched the ceiling fan blades spin until he didn't want to watch them anymore. *Sick.* The word hissed through his head. Coming from Rockwell, it was the pot calling the kettle queer. It still stung. Ron took another slug. The bourbon glowed inside him and the sting faded to a dull grey weight inside his heart.

A normal act of love. Hah. A normal act of love is with a girl, to start. Leaning against each other on the white wicker chair on her parent's veranda, where the summer winds stir the peach tree and bat their flat leaves against the porch screen while fireflies dot the blue haze of midsummer night. Listening to her talk about her typing class, and her sister's wedding, and the time she was 5 and skinned her knee on a nail. See? There's the scar. That was Vera. That was fun.

That was the closest he'd ever been to normal, him and his best friend Vera McGee, the summer all the boys in Armonk were away at war and so a high school girl like her didn't mind sitting with fatty 4-F Dickie Vleck from next door and talking about the pictures. "Do you think I look like Rita Hayworth?" she'd say, brushing her hair to one side, and he'd say "No, you look like Marion Davies," and it was true, same honey blonde ringlets and a heart shaped face.

Vera liked Joan Crawford pictures just as much as he did and so that summer they saw *When Ladies Meet* and *A Woman's Face* and *They All Kissed The Bride,* hunkered down in the red velvet seats at the Roxy, the crinkle of the wax paper bag of popcorn balanced on her shiny knees. He'd bring his stack of *Movie Star News* over to her house for the both of them to read and Vera would pretend to kiss the cover with Tyrone Power and Dickie would cringe because he'd contemplated doing the same.

"You should be a movie star," she said, tousling Dickie's hair, "you're cute, you'd be good at it," and Dickie'd blush and say "I'm too stout," and Vera said "Psssh, all it takes is exercise. Like Johnny Weissmuller—he's a swimmer." She'd drag him to the Tarzan movies, and he'd stammer and fight against the tug of her hand but secretly he screamed in delight all the way to the theater *yes, please. You Tarzan, me Dickie.* There was a cardboard standup of Weissmuller in his rawhide loincloth at the front of the lobby and the sight of him started grinding flint inside Dickie, showering sparks in a way he couldn't understand.

They sat down as the serial started: *Jimmy Lariat, Boy Wonder of the Rodeo Show*. Jimmy Lariat had a winning smile and pretty eyes and when the Injuns came they tied him up. They yanked his own lasso out of his hands and lashed it around him and when Jimmy yelped in protest they tore the red bandanna from his neck and ground it in his mouth between his teeth like a horse's bit. They *ho ho'd* and *ha ha'd* at how he struggled on the barn floor, clutching their bellies as Jimmy twisted and strained and flailed in a tight little circle, wrists bound behind his back, heels of his boots knocking together, bangs falling in his grimacing face. Dickie gripped the armrest as his breath cut into short tight gasps, in and out with the pounding pace of his heart. The Injuns were going to brand Jimmy now. They had the Lazy L iron heating white hot over the fire, and the big chief leered and grunted and pointed at Jimmy, gave the order to rip Jimmy's shirt, right across the buttons so you could see the pale virgin skin on his sweet and untouched adolescent flesh and they raised the smoking brand and suddenly something spasmed beneath Dickie's navel and in the dark of the theater all was suddenly rhapsodic and pure and scented with a thousand invisible flowers and he bent over to catch his breath. "You okay, toots?" said Vera when she saw him bend double. "Golly, they're not really going to do it. I'll tell you when it's over."

He didn't tell her and he didn't tell anyone. He went home and locked the door and lay on the bed and sweated. Jimmy Lariat swam on the blank ceiling above him, lank bangs dangling like feathers over his face, eyes bright with fear and chest naked and gag gripped between his teeth. *Don't do it*, he thought too late to stop himself. His fingers unsnapped the buttons of his fly and his hand dove, trembling, past the bramble of dark hair to the blood-hot charged velvet of the skin of his cock. *Don't do it*, he thought as his fingers gripped the shaft and a roller coaster cocktail of delight surged into his brain. Jimmy in his shirt, open to the navel, the taut muscle under his skin twitching as he struggled against his ropes. The Injun came close, hot brand in his hand. *When you burn me*, says Jimmy, *I will be yours* and the Injun brings the brand so close he can see the sweat bead in the hard gully under his throat. Jimmy, so beautiful when he's bound so tight and breathing hard and Dickie says *you will wear my mark forever* and he hovers the brand inches over his skin and Jimmy closes his eyes and there's no fear now, only knowing he's taken, he's marked, it is all so clear now, he was always meant to be for him and only him and he mouths *I love you* and suddenly the hiss of hot iron on sweat goes *tzzzzzzzzzzzzzzzzzzzzzzz—*

And Dickie gasped and shot hot pearl into the sky and the last thing he saw in his mind's eye before the shame and horror crashed down upon him was Jimmy's beautiful face thrown back and mouth open, long girlish eyelashes wet with grateful tears and the whisper on his lips said *thank you.*

He got a wilderness scout book from the library. The names of knots sounded ripe with black magic: Lark's Head, Cat's Paw, Butterfly Knot. He got twine from the shed and practiced on the bedpost, just the thickness of a young man's wrist. He penciled in ropes on the wrists and feet of Charles Atlas in the ads in the back of *Movie*

Star News, to some small thrill, but the real kick was the accompanying comic. Panel two: *Listen here*, the brute said to the kid, slim arm in his fist. *I'd smash your face—only you're so skinny you'd dry up and blow away.* In the next panel the kid griped he'd get even one day but Dickie imagined another, more dynamic conclusion. *Do it*, said the kid, *I've been waiting for my fate*, and soon he was tied like an X to the bed, torso writhing and cock throbbing in anticipation as the muscleman stoked the fire. Dickie never held out long enough to imagine what happened next.

I can make you a new man, Charles Atlas's tan face beamed and Dickie finally succumbed, sending ten cents for a book of twelve exercises. He leaned over two chairs in his bedroom and did pushups in the gulley between the seats, sweat dripping in spatters on the floor. Vera started writing to a Navy man in San Diego—"His name is Antonio but he said to call him Tony, he's swell, he's got big dreams, I think you'd like him,"—and Dickie telephoned the Y in Tarrytown and asked if they had a gym. While Vera was away he rode the bus five times a week and tossed medicine balls and skipped rope and swam lap after lap in the unheated pool. The change came in an intoxicating spurt. The muscles emerged from under melting blubber like crocuses poking their amethyst heads through a lace of spring frost. More magic words, pulsing with Latinate power: biceps, triceps, pectoralis major. Even his face sharpened, from doughy to chiseled, and the edges of his jaw and brow grew sharp and formidable, like the blade of an ax.

He loved the gym, the way the men grunted and the barbells clanked and the air was hot with sweat. He loved the sight of the new lads in the locker room, the ones who held towels shyly to their smooth chests, and he had to grit his teeth and not think too hard about what he'd like to do to them. Not that it was awful, mind you. He'd be a just master, tutoring them on the correct way to hold a barbell and heave it to the sky, how to focus the mind so that pain transmutes into something narcotic and otherworldly. How he'd shape them into something lovely—not brawny, but delicately etched with muscle—and then sign what he'd created. Heating a coat hanger with a lighter made a lovely branding iron, he'd discovered, but in a pinch a lit cigarette would do.

"Say, pal, something on my chest? You're sure staring." And Dickie blushed and swallowed hard and averted his eyes from the lithe farmboy blond three lockers down. "Just trying to remember my combination," he stammered, and the blond said "Aw, no harm done. Say, I'd sure like arms like yours. Howdya get them stovepipes?" And the bile rose in the throat of fat little nobody Dickie Vleck and he growled "Leave me alone, queer" and ran out of the room, straight into the hard chest of one of the old powerlifters, the one with the bald head and immigrant moustache. *Whummph.*

"Easy, Seabiscuit. What's the hurry?" The man grabbed his hand and pulled him up from the floor and Dickie fumbled for his breath and mumbled thanks, mortified. "Hold on now," the lifter said, putting one big hand on Dickie's chest. "You can work it off. I need a spotter." And so Dickie toddled after the man for an afternoon, watching him hoist and strain and somehow levitate layer cakes of iron weights Dickie couldn't even squint at without breaking a sweat. The old man's ropy tanned arms bulged with blood and Dickie was amazed that a man nearing 40 could be so strong.

"Your turn, sport," the man smiled, and Dickie took his place on the bench. The man stacked the bar on each side with a fearsome stack of plates and Dickie tried not to show it was more than he'd ever attempted for himself. "Don't worry," the man said with a Santa Claus smile. "I'll spot you." It was all Dickie could do to keep his head from bursting as he scraped down deep and tried to heave the monster bar back to the rack. When it finally clanked into place he gasped and looked up into in the eyes of the old powerlifter, and there was something calculating in their cold glint, like a wolf making sure he'd run all the fight out of a young deer.

"I have to get home," said Dickie, "the last bus leaves at 8."

The man held out his big hand. "Just one more thing—I've got a room here, and my dumb cluck sister sent all my things in one steamer trunk. I can't lift it by myself."

Dickie should have run when he saw the long and blank hallway, no steamer trunk in sight. "Say, where's the—," he said, too late, as the man pushed him into the room.

It was fun and not fun. It was terrifying, and exhilarating, to have this man's hands on him, and Dickie's weak fists clenched and unclenched helplessly. On the outside he was tight like an athlete but inside he was soft and girlish from a lifetime of reading and dreaming and swooning at the movies, and as the man slid his rough palms over Dickie's belly he flashed back to how it was supposed to be. Him and his angel Jimmy Lariat, the ropes and the brand and the promise of forever, not this weird wrestling match with a leathery gym Casanova old enough to be his dad. When the man pushed him to the bed and crushed him down and didn't even kiss him before yanking down the waistband of his sweatpants, his cock still jumped with the slick of the man's mouth—Jesus, is that even allowed? Is that a real thing people *do*?—Dickie jerked and gasped and succumbed in spite of himself, in a teenage minute. Before he could catch his breath the man flipped him over and introduced him to the alternative, a configuration so bizarre it took a few astonished moments for Dickie to register the pain in the ravishment. It was over in seconds, like a car wreck, and Dickie lay stunned on the bed as the man hoisted himself and retreated to the bathroom for a few mysterious minutes.

"Have a drink," the man said, and uncorked a tin flask. Dickie took a swig and swallowed, bug-eyed. It burned enough to choke, but only for a moment, and the rough edge of what pained him whittled down to blunt and bearable. He took another swig. The man gave him a stack of bills. "It's car fare," he said, the stack enough for a ride to Timbuktu and back. Dickie took it.

That's how they do it, he thought, aching in the back of the cab. The wiper blades cut the glistening rain and Dickie stared straight ahead into the black of night. He saw it now. There was normal, and there was not. Normal was being like everyone else, liking sports instead of matinees and dreaming about marriage and family with a girl like Vera. You'd buy her a ring and make a happy home together, and you'd never once stroke yourself to ecstasy over slim hipped boys tugging at their rope bonds and whispering how much they want you to burn them. *Love is the normalest thing there is*, he thought, *so if you do it with men . . . you do it without love.* He pursed his lips and said it over and over to himself. *That's how they do it. That's how they do it. That's how I do it.*

Vera came back from her trip with a tan and a crate of Pasadena clementines for her best friend. "Goll-ly, Dickie!" She took his hands and danced around him. "You're a regular Victor Mature! It's a good thing the war's over, the draft board'd take you right away!"

He almost told her. It sat in the back of his throat as she burbled about avocado trees and movie stars and highways like rivers of obsidian. He ached to let it fly from his lips, a caged wildcat of a secret that scratched and clawed and yowled to be let out. He almost told her and he couldn't. He couldn't let her face it. He could barely face himself anymore.

Tony has a plan for San Jose, she said, oblivious. *Now that the war's over he's going into real estate. He changed his name from DiPetrio to Peters. You can do that out there, you know. It's not like Armonk where you have to be so-and-so for the rest of your life.* She turned a clementine over and over in her hand and spoke the final incantation Dickie was waiting for. *Out there, you can be anyone you want.*

5

The phone cut through Ron's reverie like vinegar.

"She's waiting," said Rockwell. "DeLang's, table 7."

Ron poured another drink down his throat and put on a fresh shirt. The car man came. The drive was quick. He pushed open the quilted leather door to DeLang's and saw her table instantly: she and a handler, huddled in the sweetheart booth, and when Ron stepped up the goon vamoosed.

The upholstery was zebra and her suit was zebra too, and when she wiggled and squirmed the jostling stripes looked like a TV on the fritz. Somebody had put a comb through her hair, and a silver barrette to hold it in place. The stray tail of her peekaboo bangs still dangled into her drink. Her hazel eyes were clear and hard and she stared him down before she spoke.

"I've been on stranger dates," she said. Her voice was scuffed from screaming.

"Not me," said Ron.

A waiter swooped in with a rye for Ron—thanks, handler. She lit a cigarette with quivering hands while he downed it.

"Play nice," she scolded. "You could do worse than marrying me."

"Like what?"

"You could have your heart broken. Queers are so lucky." She put down her cigarette and lit another match, staring intently into the flame as if daring it to singe her manicure. "There's always another boy. There's always another bed." She dropped the hot charcoal squiggle onto the tablecloth. "People think I'm that way but I'm not."

"Who says that's how we operate?"

"Well, isn't it true? You ever found one you just *couldn't* let *go*?"

"Maybe."

A rubbery smile flexed across her face. "That's sweet," she said. She reached a hand inside her zebra sequined clutch purse. A little bullet tube of lipstick. "I don't care if people think it's pervy." She unscrewed a buttercream column of red and drew two plump curves on the cocktail napkin, *swoosh, swoosh*. A heart. "I think queers in love are swell." She drained her glass. "Here's the part where you tell me not to drink so much."

"Why *do* you drink so much?" he snapped.

"Why do you?" She nodded at their empty glasses. "You're staring at those dead soldiers like most men eye my rack. Let's get stinko." She raised her finger for the waiter but he grabbed her whole hand in his fist and laid it down hard on the tablecloth.

"You want to stay in Hollywood?" he said, his glare boring into her. "Or go back to the booby hatch?"

She blinked at him. "I'm not sure I know the difference," she finally slurred. "No, I think I do. In Hollywood, they let you have liquor in your private quarters." Something in her face sobered. "I'm a big girl, Ron. I know a life raft when I see one."

They were silent for a moment.

"Are you one of those queers," Lana whispered, "who doesn't like touching girls?"

"Makes no difference to me."

"All right." She twisted her hand out of his grip and twined her fingers into his. A flashbulb winked across the room, like a lightning strike in the next town over. "Let's feed the wolves."

6

DO TELL MAGAZINE NEWS FLASH: DALE DEVANCE'S SHOCKING PAST!!

Car theft, bootlegging, sordid family secrets—A NEGRO?!?

Dale DeVance, young heartthrob of TV's hit show *Spyder 550*—*colored!?!?* It's hard to imagine this rising star could be anything less than the straight-shooting race car driver detective he plays on TV's hit Thursday night show. After all, legions of his young fans have his smiling face posted in a place of honor in their bedrooms and lockers—his dimpled face looking down on them as they brush their hair for bed. But DO TELL has learned that Dale DeVance's wholesome grin hides a sinister past—a gothic tale of depravity so twisted it took all our sleuthing to uncover the grim details!

Our crack team of reporters received a tip-off from an interested party determined to set the record straight. "It disturbs me to no end," the brave whistleblower stated in an anonymous letter, postmarked "Nouvelle Orleans, Louisiana" and delivered to our offices in Santa Monica by registered courier, "that hordes of teens crowd the TV screen every Thursday night to watch Dale DeVance's character Marty Van True right wrongs and fight crimes—when everyone in Louisiana knows he's a no-good, rotten, son of a snake!"

The story starts not in New Orleans, that cultured pearl of mystery and intrigue, but in the voodoo-soaked bayous on the outskirts of Baton Rouge—a hillbilly no-man's-land of swamp people and toothless reprobates. It's here that the Laborteaux family, a Cajun clan of shiftless shadow-dwellers and con artists, have made their ill-gotten way for 5 generations. Family records are tangled and scarce, but it's known that Great-Grandpappy Guy Laborteaux owned the New Orleans underworld with an iron fist—and when his clan of cutthroats, thieves and white slavers was squeezed out of so-called "polite society," they retreated to the alligator-choked swamps to continue their dastardly ways.

The trail ends cold at the 1947 arrest record for grand theft auto and assault for Pierre "Petey" Laborteaux. It's hard to see in the sullen mug shot printed below, but look past the greasy hair and blemishes—it's none other than Dale DeVance!

Before going to press we ran this weird yarn past no other than DeVance's agent Edgar Rockwell—would he tell us the truth? "I'm sorry to confirm that everything you say is true," sighed the atomic-powered agent whose stable includes hot properties like Ron Dash, Tate McCraw, and, until recently, DeVance. "I have regretfully had to terminate DeVance's employ with my agency based on this unpleasant information," said Rockwell in a phone call, "and I will not stand for duplicity when it comes to the talent I represent."

But that's not all there is, dear readers, to this tangled, twisted tale! DO TELL's crack research team kept digging into the muck of DeVance's blackened past—and found not only a census record noting that pappy Guy lived shamefully out of matrimony with a colored woman—a light-skinned Creole slave named Jemima Gusteau—BUT THAT A LATER MARRIAGE LICENSE FOR HIS DAUGHTER—DEVANCE'S GRANDMOTHER—LISTS THE NEGRO WOMAN AS MOTHER OF THE MULATTO BRIDE!

Did *Spyder 550* co-star Jeannie Aster know about DeVance's Negro secret? A phone call to her agent only got this terse reply: "We don't

DEVANCE story continued on page 30

ON THE TOWN: What hunky Hollywood heartthrob was seen having a cozy clink of the glasses with our favorite lovely lush Lana Arleaux? None other than A NIGHT IN NIAGARA star Ron Dash, that's who!! Shutterbugs caught the juicy twosome having a quick cocktail gab (her: Kir Royale, him: rye on the rocks) in the sweetheart booth at DeLang's. Sweetheart, you say? Lana's had the love jinx ever since her smash-up divorce from pinko playright Hyman

Rabinowitz. Rumor has it she's been drowning her sorrows in tequila in dinky Mexicali dives where last month it's rumored a sore señorita challenged her to a hair-pulling match that ended them both in the pokey! Can't say for sure who sprung her bail, but Ron Dash was all ears and tears that night—even grabbing her hand in a passionate clinch at one point, onlookers say. Ladies, tell the truth—if you were a lonelyheart in need of a shoulder to cry on, wouldn't you pick the broad landing pad on tall, dark, and handsome Ron Dash? Lana's sure done worse—maybe now this soggy star will hang up the shot glasses and clean up her act for the better. Are wedding bells chiming on the horizon again for three-time loser Lana and never married man-about-town Dash? As soon as DO TELL knows—you will too!

Correction: In our previous issue (Feb '57) we reported on Ron Dash and Grayson Todd involved in a questionable all-male party. The story was planted by Communists. We regret the error.

7

We regret the error. Sunday was bright and amnesiac, but Saturday night still pounded in Ron's head. He held his aching brow under the hot spray of shower water. *Yes, we regret.* There was new soap in this hotel room, and a razor. "Okay if I use this?" he called back to the bedroom. No answer. He lathered up and leaned his head out the door. "Hey fella, okay if I use—"

The bed was unmade. The room was empty. The key was on the nightstand. A note: *Crane's, lunch, Rockwell,* pinned to the suit in the dry cleaning bag hung from the top of the door. The suit fit fine but Ron was in no mood for fancy dress. He scowled in the driver's seat all the way from Venice Beach to Ventura, to the green and white awning of Joe Crane's Cafe, the key burning a hole in his pocket.

Rockwell was already seated. "You look refreshed," he said as he clapped Ron on the back. "March is springtime enough for gin and tonnies, right?" He smiled as they took their seats. "It's a nice day. Let's pretend we're at Wimbledon. G&T for me, *garçon*."

"Bourbon," said Ron. He wanted to fling the key on the table but decided to wait until he had a drink in him.

Rockwell clucked his tongue. "A foolish consistency, et cetera." He unfolded the menu. "I like the Cobb Salad here. It's not as good as at the Brown Derby, but still . . ." He folded the menu again and placed it under his hands, gravely. "Grayson Todd is taking a spiritual retreat back to Kentucky. He'll be returning to his family's compound for three months of prayer and reflection. "

Ron raised an eyebrow. "And his work?"

"On hold. While he rebaptizes himself and sweats some of that spunk out of his pores. Which means I need to find someone to fill his bathing trunks for the two beach movies remaining on his contract."

"A new face."

"Naturally. Can you recommend anyone?"

Ron knew what Rockwell was asking: *how was that piece of trade I got to babysit you last night? Blond enough? Butch enough? Does he take direction? I thought you might be lonely. Lonely men do foolish things.* Ron could have sworn he'd gone outside Rockwell's hunting range, too. No one from the backlot cruised as far out as Venice, out to the nameless door that hid the beatnik bar that hid the damp cruising ground in the basement. The milk-fed choirboy leaning on the jukebox should have rung Ron's warning bells: *too good to be true.*

"You're the one with the legendary eye," Ron said to Rockwell. "I'm not paid to spot new faces."

When he put a quarter in the machine the kid did a double take. "Gee, you know who you look like?"

Ron smiled and said "I wish I had his life." Then he turned on his heel and retreated up the stairs to the bar. He was taking out his car keys when the kid appeared behind him. "Golly, I'm sorry, mister. If you're going, could you give me a lift?" The honeypot was perfect: He was minding a motel for his stepfather. His buddies ditched him here. Ron wouldn't have taken the bait if the kid hadn't dug a full ring of motel keys out of his jeans. "How far away is it?" he heard himself asking.

"Well, anyone can spot a real star," said Rockwell. "If you have it, you have it."

"You want some reefer?" the kid asked from the front seat. They were on the boulevard. Ron passed him his lighter. "Up on the right," he croaked as he passed Ron the joint. A low, squat motel with a NO VACANCY sign. "I'm just supposed to turn it on at night so they'll leave us alone," the kid said. "My uncle doesn't want anyone around while he's gone."

The kid fumbled with the ring but they were inside just as the thoughts in Ron's head started to swirl like silk scarves in water. "Where are you from?" he asked. "Des Moines," the kid said as he stripped off his shirt. The thoughts crowded for the runway of Ron's tongue. He finally spoke. "How do we get lost here?" Then, another thought, as the kid's supple body lay beneath him: "Do you want me to pay you?"

"No," the kid said. "it's not like that." And then the tears came unbidden to Ron's eyes. "There was a Mexican," he started, and then the thoughts came piling in: the broken nose, the coffee shop brush-off, Dale DeVance dying for his sins. "I think I've done something terrible."

"Shhh," the kid said, and Ron said "Why don't you go back home?" and as soon as he said it he knew how pointless it was to steer someone young away from this place, no matter how broken he knew this town would make him. The kid said, "Go home? Hell no, mister, I'm ready for anything new." And something snapped loose from the mooring and Ron's mouth watered as he said "Then hand me a cigarette."

The waiter returned with salads heaped with bright orange dressing. Ron scooted the leaves around with a fork while Rockwell ate.

"Some people are born stars," Rockwell continued, "and others are nothing without the proper buildup. Speaking of which—Dale DeVance was released from his contract this morning," Rockwell said, dabbing the corner of his mouth. "And so were you."

Ron blanched as white as the hearts of palm on his plate. That was it. It was over. Five pictures in four years, shared billing with his lead, script approval and no loanouts to other studios, $700 a week plus the mortgage on his mansion. Dale DeVance takes a dive but the damage was already done. Was it done last night? Had Rockwell set him up for one last test, to see if he could resist indiscreet pickings? Or was that Iowa farmboy—if that's even who he was—the equivalent of the condemned man's choice of a last meal? Did Rockwell arrange for the kid to leave the key so he'd have somewhere to lay his head the first night he was run out of town?

"Jesus, Rock," he hyperventilated. "I thought you took clients to Crane's for good news."

"I do." Rockwell extended his hand. "They tore it up and I signed you a new one. Two grand a week. Beach house in Malibu. New Coupe De Ville. Billing over your co-star. And you're getting the first picture in that British spy novel property they just bought. Hot stuff." He raised his glass. "Congratulations, kid. You're Ultimate's favorite son." He winked. "So who are you going to tell first?"

8

"Chateau Montserrat, Beverly Hills," trilled the woman on the phone. "Good morning."

"Good morning." Ron twirled a cigarette in his fingers as he spoke into the phone. "I'm a former guest, I'm looking to speak to one of your employees."

"Is there a problem, sir?"

"No, no problem. I owed him a tip and didn't get it to him."

"What's his name?"

"Um . . ." Ron put his fingers to his temples and thought hard. "Not sure. Wait—Franco? He was an elevator boy. He's Mexican."

"You need to tip an elevator boy?" The voice on the other end of the line lilted upwards, confused.

"He helped the porter with some of my bags. I want to make sure he wasn't overlooked."

"Just a moment, sir." The click of the headset placed down on the desk, footsteps walking away. Hushed voices. Ron tapped his cigarette on the tabletop and took a deep, shaky breath. The butterflies in his stomach wouldn't quit.

Heavy footsteps, coming closer. A different, deep voice. "Good afternoon, sir, this is the day manager. How may I help you?"

"Um . . " Ron swallowed hard. "I'm trying to get in touch with one of your employees?"

"And whom may I say is calling?"

Shit. "Uh—my name is Ron Dash. I'm a former guest of your h—"

"Mr. Sandoval is no longer in our employ." The voice grew frosty. "There was an incident. I'm sure you understand."

"Yes, of course." Ron bit his lip. "I do understand. Thank you for your help."

"Not at all, Mr. Dash. Please come again." The man hung up before Ron did.

There was a notepad nearby. Ron wrote in careful script: *Franco Sandoval*. He stared at his words for a moment. Suddenly it came back to him, in a wash of recollection like a sudden breeze. He crossed out the first name and wrote *Flaco*.

He opened the phone book and started paging through. There were Sandovals in Boyle Heights. Family? He couldn't call—what would he say? How would he explain himself? But he could drive down, some sunny afternoon, and there he would be, dressed in crisp elevator boy whites on the corner of Soto and Alcazar. They would drive to

Mulholland Highway, where the HOLLYWOOD sign is so close it feels like you can touch it, and he would say "Should we stop here and look around?" and Flaco would say "No, drive further, further, as far as you can go—"

The phone's jangle shattered his reverie.

Ron picked up. "Hello?"

"H'lo?" slurred a high and startled voice.

"Lana?"

"Whoozit?" The sound of things sliding off a night table and crashing to the floor.

"It's Ron."

"Oh, Ron. *Hiiiii*, Ron." The voice dropped an octave to a cultured, measured purr. Ron heard the *fssh* flare of a lighter. "How's my favorite fake fiancé doing?"

"You're starting early."

"Haven't had my coffee. I want to come over for a drink? See the house? The publicity people shoot our engagement portrait on Monday, I want to pretend I've been there before." She blew a mouthful of smoke. "Did you get good news too?"

"Two thousand a week. The British spy pic."

"Mm-hmm. Supremity Pictures reinstated me. No morals clause, either." She spoke the words with care, as if it was a tower of teacups she might overturn. "I'm back on that frontier drama, thanks to you."

"Thanks to our agents."

"Right. The zookeepers." She exhaled again. "I'm not dressed. Give me an hour?"

"It's not formal. Come as you are."

"Mmm, don't think you want *that*. An hour. See you." She hung up.

He was straightening the pillows on the sofa when the doorbell rang. He answered it. She looked tiny as a lawn ornament on the front doorstep, nipped waist suit and big black sunglasses and swirl of blonde hair like cake batter drizzling from a spoon. Ron guessed she barely cracked five feet tall out of her platform heels.

"You're early," he said.

"I despise lateness," she said, smoothing her hair with her gloved hands. "Being late means missing something." She stepped over the threshold. "May I?"

"Please." He crossed the room to the bar. "I don't have champagne. I know you like Kir Royales."

"Something sweet, then. And mean." She took off her sunglasses and Ron saw the dark halo ringing her left eye.

"Jesus," he said. "Who gave you that shiner?"

"I did. I walked into the broomstick while mopping the floor. Put some potato juice in that." Ron splashed vodka atop the shot of peach schnapps before handing the tumbler to her. She took it gratefully. "I like to get drunk before doing housework because it's such a drag otherwise."

"What about your maid?"

"Don't have one. Maids are proletariats. I'm a proletariat too. I'm a worker at the whim of bigger forces. I'm only paid like a bourgeoisie." She sipped. "When I'm all done with this town I'm moving to Cuba. I've been sending money there for years. A collective farm and orphanage in Mayabeque has a cot all ready for me, with a picture of

Marx hanging above my pillow." She looked at him. "Does that shock you?"

"A little."

"Good." She smiled. "Now we both have a secret."

She sat on the couch and kicked her heels against the couch. Her feet barely scuffed the floor. "Gee, mister," she said, eyeing the surroundings. "You sure have a nice place."

"The studio bought it for me."

"Did they buy that for you too?" She pointed to the painting over the hearth's mantelpiece, a black square hovering over a smaller red square. The red square hung at a playful tilt and the black square stood watch, like a sentry.

"That's mine."

"It's not a real Malevich, is it?"

"It's a copy. I'm impressed you know Malevich."

"I know all the revolutionaries."

He sat down next to her, drink in hand. "I saw the real one in a museum. I paid a painting student at UCLA fifty bucks to make me another one."

"A big black square and a little red square." She shot him a look, eyes twinkling. "You're the black square. On top, right? And where would I find the red square?"

"Moscow, I believe."

"Okay. Don't tell your wife." She smiled. "I'll buy you a painting of St. Sebastian shot full of arrows and lashed to a tree as a wedding gift. And when guests come over you can tell them it's mine, and I'm very, very Catholic." She put her drink on the table and stood up. "Come on," she said, extending her hand. "Show me where I'm staying."

"You've got your choice," said Ron as he led her up the stairs. "There's the white room." He flicked on the light. White down coverlet, ostrich feathers in alabaster urns, Art Nouveau vanity in curling chrome silver, milky canopy ceiling dotted with glass beads. "Or the red room." He gestured across the hall. Crimson drapes, eggplant black jaguar sculpture, a big round bed as plush and scarlet as a ripe plum cut in half.

"Ooh!" She squealed and clapped her hands. "I like the red room. I have a leopard skin rug named John The Baptist. He'll look just peachy there. That all right?"

He nodded.

"Where do you sleep?" she asked.

"Down the hall."

"Can I see it?"

He hesitated. "Sure."

"I don't have to."

"It's all right." He lifted the sconce on the hall table and palmed a small brass key. He could feel her eyes following his back as he bent to turn the lock. He braced himself for it, waiting for the quick snap of the wisecrack making note of what kind of man locks his bedroom when he's away. It never came. He turned and looked at her. Her eyes were kind and pale and free of judgment, soft topaz pools ringed by a Pete the Pup bruise.

He pushed open the door.

She walked through the threshold carefully, picking over the pewter carpet in her heels like a deer stepping into a frosty meadow. He saw his *sanctum sanctorum* afresh through her newcomer's eyes. Slate grey walls, dark as pencil lead. Black duvet on onyx bed. Ebony wood cabinets lining the walls, tall and impassive as a butler and yielding no secrets past their locked keyholes. Neat, solemn, sterile. *Tomblike*, Ron realized with a shock.

"No brick hearth." She smiled. "No guns, no beer steins. No hunt lodge taxidermy."

"Not my thing."

"What, you don't like making love with a disembodied moose head leering over you? You *must* be queer." She ran her finger over the surface of the dresser. "Spotless, too. But the help isn't allowed in here. So you know how to keep house. Good for you." She looked up. The vault of the ceiling was stenciled with a firmament of twinkling constellations, real hammered silver leaf burnished on indigo fresco. Flat California daylight dimmed the stars to mere glints. Ron wondered if she'd notice them. She did.

"Stars . . ." she said, soft exhalation full of enchantment.

"At night they catch the headlights of cars passing outside," said Ron. "They're hard to see in daylight, but you found them."

"They say war orphans draw pictures full of stars," said Lana. She twirled under the ceiling in sleepy pirouettes, eyes bright, head craned up like a Sistine Chapel tourist. "That's how their caretakers know they've turned the corner. Stars mean hope and yearning for better things. I don't like it when people call me a star." She ducked her chin down. "I don't think I deserve the comparison." Her face clouded like tornado weather. For one dark moment Ron thought she would crumple like a beer can. Then something sharpened her mask. She pulled the corners of her lacquered lips into a fiberglass smile and turned to him.

"Let's see it."

"See what?"

"Your dirty books."

A little blush rose to Ron's cheeks. "I'm afraid I don't know what you're talking about."

"Don't play dumb. Are they in the cabinets or under the bed?"

"Pornographic photos are illegal."

"And you're Joe Law." She flicked at the nearest cabinet's knob with her fingernail. "Come on. I want to see them."

"Why?"

"Because I like dirty pictures." She gave him a bashful grin. "I like them," she repeated, her transatlantic contralto suddenly coy and baby-meek.

The Easter chick fluff in her voice melted his hesitance. He unlocked the cabinet and unearthed the fat accordion folder hidden on the bottom shelf. She sprawled out on the bed, dangling ankles winding in clockwork circles in anticipation as he unfolded the heavy leather flap and extracted the first packet of pamphlets with ecclesiastical care. *Physique Illustrated*, the Palmer Method script read in a hand-drawn arc above the top magazine's cover photo. An oiled bodybuilder reclined like the Barberini Faun in wool knit swim trunks. *Aesthetic Fitness League, Los Angeles*.

There were thirty magazines in the stack, thirty sets of chests and navels and thumbtack nipples and parted thighs. Lana pawed at the pamphlets eagerly, spreading them out on the satin bedspread like a casino dealer fanning out a lascivious poker hand. "Where did you get these?" she gasped, eyes as big as other women gaping at diamond baubles.

"They call them fitness magazines," said Ron, sidestepping the question. He tapped his finger on one photo, right at the minimal loincloth binding up the boy's privates. "As long as there's no nudes, they can send them through the mail." She nodded, hand still stroking the cover's glossy surface. Ron watched her. There was no idle curiosity in her gaze, no jaded continental thrill of being the sort of girl who likes what other girls don't. He saw how carefully she took in each man's proportions, the way the lumps of muscle undulated under the skin, girding humble bones into something Grecian and immortal. Something went quiet in her face. Ron suddenly noticed the freckles sprinkling the bridge of her nose and the twiggy laugh lines etched at the corners of her unblackened eye. The movie star came to the door, but here, vulnerable and prostrate at the mouth of her own desire, she became suddenly human.

"There's more," he said, emboldened by her hunger. He opened another fold and lifted out a stack of black-and white 8x10s, the photo emulsion shiny like baby oil. Her eyes grew wide but she didn't flinch. These were the harder stuff, Bakersfield gas station boys and West Hollywood carhops and Long Beach dock workers, gay for a day while some sweaty fool squatted behind the camera and told them to smile more. It pained Ron a little to own photos like these because he knew the drill.

"I wish I were a man," Lana moaned, stroking her fingers on the photo's surface. "It's so much easier. So few rules."

"It's not," said Ron, his thoughts suddenly tangled in the sour milk taste of a memory. An unheated garage, holding your breath between shots so the vapor wouldn't show on the negative. The lanky mechanic standing before him: red hair crinkled in Persian lamb rows, gibbon arms dotted with chigger-bite track marks. Button fly, smelling like motor oil and musk. He shot Dickie a look of furious contempt for the crime of allowing his mouth to harbor the flood of his semen. Dickie took his fifty bucks—the other boy only got thirty—and got the hell out of there, outracing the menace-tinged cries of the kid whose cum still roughened the surface of Ron's teeth. *Hey. Hey, you. I want to talk to you a minute.*

"Did you do this, once upon a time?" said Lana, reading his thoughts.

"I did." Something dawned on him. "Did you?"

"Mm. Not really." She lifted one photo carefully in her porcelain hands. A varsity swimmer bent over a table. A sailor on leave, behind. It wasn't clear if the anchor scrawled on his bicep was tattoo ink or eyeliner. It was very clear how his hands spread the swimmer's cheeks and the glistening tip of his torpedo cock split the pucker of his quarry's ass. "I was an artist's model in Santa Cruz. Fine art, not photos. That means someone wants to make you their muse. It helped with the bills. I didn't think of it that way at the time." She put the photo down. "When Supremity bought me they bought all his work. I watched them burn it out by Backlot C." Her voice dropped to a childlike hush. "I hate the smell of oil paint on fire. It's *metallic*." She pronounced the last word with clicking contempt, then laid the picture down on the bedspread, gesturing with one finger like a lecturer's baton. "Big square," she said softly, pointing to the sailor. "Little square," she said about the boy beneath him.

Ron held his tongue for a moment, and then spoke.

"That room you were in," he started. "That's where my manager Rockwell takes all the new ones." He lifted another photo from the stack. A gymnasium. Padded floor, hanging bag, two way mirror along one side. Two college boys at the bag. Shorts around their thighs, jockstraps pushed to the side. Fists gripped around each other's flagpole cocks. "That's where he auditions them. Some he likes and some he doesn't. The ones he likes a little he keeps for his photo business. The ones he likes a lot he puts in the movies. He liked me a lot, and he adopted me. And then I became Ron Dash. It's not a real gym," he continued, pointing to the punching bag. "It's just a set. But I guess he put you there because the floor's real padding. He didn't want you to hurt yourself."

Lana shook her head, vaguely. "I don't remember."

Ron looked at her, incredulous. "I remember," he said. "They had you in a straitjacket. You screamed like someone was beating your mother to death. You really don't recall?"

She shook her head. "Don't feel bad," she said, eyes so calm it scared Ron. "It's not the first time."

Ron didn't know what to say about that. Lana, unconcerned, stretched out on the bed, hands folded over her belly like a country girl lazing in the grass. Ron lay down next to her. The tops of their heads almost touched.

"Am I the first girl who's ever seen this bedroom?" said Lana.

"I think so."

"Am I the first girl who's ever seen your bedroom, period?"

"I get what you're angling for."

"I'm not interested in setting you right. I'm just curious." She stared at the ceiling, the stars dotted in silver leaf on the indigo sky.

"Not idly curious, though." She sat up on one elbow and looked at him. "I want you to know something," she said, her voice suddenly stripped of its flirtation. "I might have been married three times. But I took it seriously each time. And even though we're not—" Her face twisted as she stumbled for the precise words—"we're not *lovers*," she finally spoke, "I take this just as seriously."

Ron froze. "I hope you're not in love with me."

"That's a hard question to answer when you put it like that." She flounced back down on the bed. "If I say 'yes', then you panic and if I say 'no' it still stings. So I'll put it my way instead." She extended her crooked little pinky. "We can make a good team."

He looked at her for a moment. Then he extended his own pinky and linked with hers. They shook on it. Lana sighed and folded her hands on her belly.

"I like you, Ron." She smiled. "I think I won't mind being married to you."

9

The bride wore lavender. It was her little joke, and Ron didn't mind. The flashbulbs sparked and champagne corks popped as they cut the towering white cake together. The morsel she placed in his mouth was sweet.

In the receiving line Darkroom Louie pressed a twenty into Lana's hand with a wink and said "Swell shindig, Mrs. Ronald H. Dash." Then, aside, in Ron's ear, "We all know what the H stands for. But why ruin a beautiful day with the details?" He lifted his camera. "Smile for the birdie, lovebirds."

Fsssh.

It was a beautiful day. Darkroom Louie couldn't ruin it. Lana threw the bouquet and Ron watched Gayla Sheer from Supremity and Margot Moreau from Ultimate and Vera Van Buren from All-Patriot Studios rush for the puffball of nasturtiums in a cavalcade of squeals. Rockwell shook the groom's hand and said, loud enough for everyone to hear,

"It's my pleasure to give this happy couple a week's respite from their motion picture obligations for the honeymoon they deserve." Ron had no way to know if he meant it, and didn't care. The fizz of champagne tickled his nose.

Rockwell did mean it. Plane tickets and packed bags waited in the foyer of Ron's home with a bowling pin magnum of champagne. "Trans World Airlines," Lana read, shuffling through the ream of tickets. "Los Angeles to Kansas City. Kansas City to New York. New York to Niagara Falls." She grinned. "Let's ditch 'em."

They threw the bags into her Nash Rambler and piled in, California Route 1 as far as it would take them. She'd shed her dress for a peasant blouse and khakis, the magnum of champagne clutched between her tiny thighs. The sunset lolled on their right like a fiery scoop of sherbet melting in the sky. The further south they drove the radio got mean and loud, thumping colored music crowding over Perry Como and Pat Boone in a switchblade crush of static. "It's the border stations," shouted Lana. "They play rock and roll." *A wop bop a lu bop a wop bam boom.*

She knew just where to go in Tijuana—Tres Diablesas, a two-story cantina cozying up to the border, the froth of its stucco the same rich white swirls as the icing on their wedding cake. The sign said "NO MUJERES" but the barkeep spotted Lana and waved both of them into the seething heat of the dining room, winding through chockablock tables and stubbly desperadoes hunkered over sweating mugs of *cerveza* and pudgy mariachis hoisting shopworn guitars. They put plates down before Ron, tacos with gristly meat and fresh lime, and when he took a bite Lana gasped and burbled. "It's pig ear! I should have warned you." No worry. It was savory and good and the tumbler of tequila at his wrist took away all his fear. She ate with both hands, burbling in Spanish to the barkeep when he came to check on her. "Muy bien, Carlito!" she squealed. "Sooooo very muy bien." She put her hand on Ron's shoulder. "Él es mi marido," she shouted. The man clapped Ron on the back.

The night passed in a blur of red and gold: the cups of vermillion and scarlet and emerald salsa clustered on the table like presents hunched under a Christmas tree, the toothless matron with sharp penciled eyebrows wailing sad songs at the door until Lana waved her and her concertina accompanist inside, the strange trio croaking out the Internationale. "*Agrupémonos todos, en la lucha final. El género humano es la internacional.*" The voodoo-scented slick of tequila washing down his throat, the punchline of chickens pecking at his ankles beneath the table. Lana dancing, Lana laughing, Lana downing another shot and triumphantly slamming the empty glass on the table. Lana, the same colors as this place, red lips and gold hair and topaz tiger eyes glittering like a bonfire. Red and gold and alive.

They stumbled upstairs to their room above the cantina, a square concrete room with two sad cots cowering like accident victims against the azure walls. Lana threw herself on one bed with a pained squeak of bedsprings. The metal pull chain on the bare light bulb made three maddening feints away from Ron's drunken hand before he caught it in his palm. He turned off the light and crashed on his bed the same way, a symphony of complaining metal greeting his weight.

The dark of the room still spun with tequila whirlies, the carnival hubbub of downstairs a distant roar beneath the floor. "Are you all right here?" whispered Lana in the dark. "Yes," said Ron, and he meant it.

Morning came with crushing suddenness. Ron's hangover filled his head with the vengeance of a loan shark coming for what's due. Lana sat at the edge of the bed, clutching the bed frame like an undecided suicide peering over the edge of the bridge. A spray of hangover sweat christened her face like fairy dust. "Let's get eggs," she rasped.

"Don't say eggs," moaned Ron, but moments later they were downstairs again, seated before piled high plates of salsa-smothered *huevos rancheros* and mugs of Dos Equis, ambrosial and cold. A fat woman the color of milk chocolate stood behind the bar and patted tortilla dough between her enormous palms. Ron ate and drank and slowly the throb of blood in his temples faded to the soft *pat pat pat* of her rhythm, like a consoling hand on the shoulder. *There, there.*

They walked down Avenida Revolucion arm in arm like millionaires on promenade, bright Tijuana sun glinting starlike inside his dark glasses. Hustlers, barkers, shopkeepers, vendors, chickens, half-naked cinnamon children dusty as sugar cookies, all-naked pigs sunburned and grunting. A bored donkey, its shaggy fur caked with black and white witch stocking stripes, one dollar for your photo astride *la zebra*. Everyone hectoring loud and hot for *gringo* money like tropical flowers screaming fragrance for honeybee attention. Ron's heart pulsed, the decadent sleepwalker stride of the deliciously hungover.

"I've had honeymoons before," said Lana. "They're not much fun. You run back to the hotel in your crinkly clothes and make sure to consecrate what you've done with one big fuck. Not for fun. Just stamping your thumbprint at the bottom of the contract. To convince yourself that you're not in trouble. To fool yourself that you're not in a marriage so doomed you didn't even fuck the first night." She sighed. "Then you wake up the next day and look at each other and say 'Well, what do you want to do today?' Because neither of you has any idea anymore." She hugged his arm with both hands. A wooden fruit cart clattered by on big-spoked wheels, China red crates overladen with guavas, mangos, Muscat grapes like wet jade marbles. "But I don't feel like that with you. I like that."

"You know the town better. Makes no sense for me to play tour guide."

"It's not just that." She hugged his arm closer. "Maybe it's because you're queer, but here with you, I feel like I can behave like myself. Like a man behaves. Beholden only to his whims." She fluttered her fingers through the air like butterflies.

They were crossing the street now, off the main drag and into the carnal sideshow of the Zona Norte—the flesh peddlers district. Women were everywhere, young and old, *frijoles*-fattened curves crammed into tight skirts and feet wedged into fuck-me heels. They leaned against every store and theater like flying buttresses, as if the combined

69

strength of their scabby legs was all that kept the walls from crashing down on the herd of horny sailors and pimps and opportunists swarming through the streets. One yellow wall was lined with males, not females, and Ron felt the boy hustlers honing in on his frequency as they walked past. Two dozen pairs of dark eyes locking on him, narrow hips and skinny shoulders turning towards him like cat's ears following a skitter in the baseboards. They saw right through Ron and Lana together and he knew it. Breakfast soured in his stomach and he swallowed hard.

Lana saw them staring, too. "You can look," she cooed. "Even a Bolshevik like me slows down when I pass the window at Tiffany's."

"I don't like it," said Ron. Something curdled and raw was rising up in him. The beers he'd had for breakfast suddenly weren't enough. A drink, strong. Soon. *Now*. His jaw clenched and his temples throbbed.

"I don't judge prostitutes," she continued breezily. "With my job, I've got no moral high ground. Besides, from each according to his ability, to each according to his needs."

"Then you should buy a boy for yourself." The headache was full force now, the boa constrictor wrapped tight around his skull and unhinging its jaws to swallow his head whole. He rubbed his temples and prayed for vodka rain.

"Not for me." She shook her head. " I fall in love too hard to fuck around. It's just a woman's way. I wish I *were* a man. So few rules. So few consequences."

"Says you."

"I do." She looked at him hard over her sunglasses. "Try and live like a girl sometimes. Can't curse, can't fuck, can't get mad like a man. The world puts you on a pedestal and knots a noose around your throat. Stepping down means snapping your neck." She slapped his shoulder hard, to his annoyance. "Then go back to Boy's Town and see how much dead brush those big broad shoulders can push out of your way. Like an elephant crashing through the jungle."

"What do you think my life is like?" said Ron, incredulous. He stopped and stared at her. "How do you think I live?"

"I think you fuck whomever you want," she enunciated carefully. "And that big truth cuts through your life like an ocean liner and leaves a wake wide enough to hold anything else you need . . ." She trailed off, eyes vague at the magnitude of something grand and unseen.

Anger flared inside Ron in a spiraling spurt of fireworks. He shrugged off her arm. "You're wrong," he spat, staring her down. "You are goddamn wrong."

"I'm not wrong. Straight boys kiss and tell but faggots keep each other's secrets," she said. Beer soured her tone. "Isn't that your little brotherhood? You screw each other like alley cats on the ground floor and the men watching in the balcony protect you. But when girls like me fall hard it's nothing but a basket of nettles six stories down. There's no fairy godmother to cushion my ass. You don't know how good you have it."

"It is not like that at all," said Ron. The words tumbled out of his mouth as if conjured by demons. "You are drunk and you are a bitch and you are goddamn wrong about men, and about me, and about everything."

"You're drunk, too." Her eyes flashed like burning sugar. "Bitch is just another man's opinion. But faggot is what you are. Go ahead and hit me," she said, her voice rising in challenge. "That'll get my fourth honeymoon off to the start it deserves."

He turned and stalked away, storming upstream against a tide of street hawkers, back to who knows where. Her words smouldered in the tinder of his hangover and suddenly burst into flame. He spun on his heel and slapped her, hard, the sudden snap of her head throwing her hair into the air in a peacock-tail spray of gold, her sunglasses clattering to the ground.

"Goddamn you," she hissed, but she didn't look mad. She looked exhilarated as she pressed her palm to her pinkening cheek.

Ron looked at her, and something deflated dead inside him.

"I'm sorry," he babbled, and then suddenly burst into tears.

There, in the middle of the Mercado, was Ron Dash, he-man of the silver screen, fists in his eyes like a crybaby, racking with sobs that dug deep out of him in great heaving gasps. Tears falling in the dirt beneath him like birdshit splatters. Slapping a woman didn't draw a crowd in the mean Zona Norte, but the sight of a gringo man with his face contorted like a Greek mask in tears formed a magnetic north for the crowd's macho disdain. Pachucos in zoot suit pants and shiny shoes nodded and winked and sniggered at him. Ron didn't speak the slurs and didn't have to. "Ay, *puto*," "*Puñal*," "*Maricón*," "*El joto*." He was 14 years old again, standing impotent over soggy movie magazines knocked in the gutter. *Crybaby, crybaby, crybaby Dickie. He likes boys 'cuz he's a little sickie.*

"What?" Lana stood next to him, mouth agape, hand still glued to the palm print on her cheek. "What . . . ?"

Ron grabbed her by the shoulders and pulled her into an alleyway, up against the dirty brick wall. He held her there, hands gripping her forearms, unable to look her in the eye as he told her. He told her everything. Dickie Vleck and Johnny Weismuller. The Y in Armonk and the handlebar moustache man and the taxi ride home. The bus ride to Hollywood. The crinkle-haired boy and the baking soda taste of his cum. The photos that landed on Rockwell's desk. How he landed on Rockwell's desk too, belt buckle knocking against his knees as the old man hissed in his ear with each thrust how he'd make him a star. The lessons in how to walk and sit and talk like a normal man, the rechristening as Ron Dash. The build-up, the fan magazines, the whitewash complete. The bourbon that got him out of bed each morning and the vodka that got him to sleep. The swell stag fag parties in Hollywood Hills where men did fuck like alley cats, just as she suspected, except the men in the balcony only cared enough to save what was pink-cheeked and firm and could still spin cum into gold for their pockets.

The Judas job of Dale DeVance. Everything that led up to the sham marriage here, the sham honeymoon that was the latest notch in his sham life. And finally, the boy in the hotel, tawny skin and rumpled sheets, and how he bought his scandal away with a sticky bun and a fistful of cash. Ruining someone, just how he was ruined. He left out how he liked his Mexican bound and gagged and burned with cigarettes, but the rest was truth. She listened, rapt, eyes growing wider and wider, head shaking back and forth with incredulous twitches, as if being slapped again.

"Jesus," she finally gasped. "Jesus, you poor fool."

"I know," sobbed Ron. He hovered over her, framing her head with the vulture hunch of his bowed head. "A poor fool." He said it again and it became more true. "A poor and goddamned fool."

The pachucos were sniggering and giggling now, chattering in meathead Spanish, daring each other to make trouble with this sissy gringo and the pretty girl he was holding hostage. A police officer saw them and waved his billy club. They scattered like pigeons in a flutter of chino. Then the officer saw the big man bent over the pretty white girl and took his club out again.

Lana saw him approaching before Ron did. "*Todo esta bien, señor.*" She smiled and waved. "It's okay." The officer eyed her warily and finally backed away.

Lana took Ron's hands from his face. She clutched them in her own, her slim white fingers binding his trembling hands.

"I hit you," shuddered Ron. "I've never hit a woman my entire life."

"I forgive you," said Lana.

"You shouldn't."

"I've been hit before." She put her finger under his chin and tilted his eyes to meet hers. "I know the kind you forgive and the kind you don't. Come on," she said. "Let's go to the races."

10

They drove down Agua Caliente Boulevard, 3 miles of blue sky. Lana drove, white hands on the red leather steering wheel. Ron slumped in the front seat and let the wind wash his face. They sat in the grandstands, half in and half out of the sun. She bought him a margarita from the boy vendors, lime and tequila and Triple Sec shaken up in a waxed paper cup. He took it gratefully. The salt clung to his lips and stung like his aggravated conscience. Tequila numbed his shame enough to settle into the racetrack's rhythm, cyclic as clockwork: the ebullient announcements in Spanish, the klaxon of bugles, the crash of the gates and the howl of the crowd. Another phalanx of horses, streaming out in a solid thunderous wave of churning hooves and straining necks, jockeys in silks bobbing overarching black backs like confetti floating on an oil slick. "Come on, Carlito, *mi cariño*," Lana yelled, cheering not for the sleek horse but the rider astride him. Carlito in holly green silks thundered across the finish and Lana whooped in shared triumph. Ron smiled. It seemed right for her to win.

Lana's tickets were pink and handwritten and thin as tissue, not cracker-tan cardboard stamped with purple ink like the slips issued at the official betting booth. She waved her tickets in a fan as they wound their way down to the jockey yard, down where the fat and stubbly horse trainer with the hedgehog face grinned when he saw Lana coming. He didn't break his smile even when reaching into his apron for Lana's cash. Pesos still looked like play money to him but Ron was still stunned to see a ream of cash so thick in the man's hands. "You just emptied this guy out," said Ron. "Why's he so happy to pay?"

"Because I just bought them a horse." She smiled at the horse trainer as he counted out pesos between his fat fingers. "They pay me for the race. But I made a side bet that if Carlito beat his best time, I'd buy him the horse he wanted. *Este?*" she said, pointing to the chestnut animal placidly gnawing hay in the next stall. "*Si,*" the trainer smiled, fat belly rocking with mirth.

The jockey Carlito came around the corner, breathless and sweaty as the horse he just rode. His compatriots clapped him on the back. Ron marveled at how you could break a sweat just sitting atop an animal, but the butterflies of sweat graying his cotton undershirt testified to its effort. When Carlito's eyes met Lana his eyebrows jumped with recognition and she hugged him like a brother. Ron noticed he was barely taller than she was and probably not heavier, but his arms were strong and ropy and his mahogany face was lined like a man's. He could be older than either of them, easily—or he could be younger than anyone with a face so weathered deserved to be.

"You've got your horse," Lana smiled. "What are you going to name her? ¿Qué nombre?"

"La Corderita." Carlito smiled, a broad grin that exposed his horsey teeth. "*Que es la única corderita que proviene de la lana.*" Lana threw back her head and laughed.

"What's so funny?" said Ron.

"La Corderita" means 'little lamb.' He said it's the only lamb that came from wool—from *lana*—instead of the other way around." Carlito grinned broadly, delight shining on his face.

"They work hard here," continued Lana, as Carlito's amigos continued to clap him on the back and ruffle his hair as if he were a lucky Buddha. "It's a backbreaking life—quite literally, sometimes. And they never own the means of their production. So I want to change that. I've known Carlito since he was *muy pequeño.*"

"*Yo siempre he sido muy pequeño.*"

Lana laughed again. "He says he's still small. *Los regalos buenos vienen en paquetes pequeños.*" Carlito laughed and Ron got the gist.

Lana and Carlito bantered happy and light in cartwheeling Spanish while Ron looked around the stable. Four walls of gritty concrete, chipped paint and drains in the floor, heady with the whiff of manure and straw and sweat. A holding pen for anonymous laborers, men who couldn't get Lana a room at The Ambassador or a table at The Cocoanut Grove, who didn't even fawn and swoon over her china doll looks but instead chatted and laughed and stood eye to eye like factory workers on cigarette break. They didn't treat her like a screen goddess because she didn't act like one. She was human, Ron realized. True, complete, realer than anyone he'd ever known.

The last person who came close was Vera. But Vera didn't know all his secrets. Lana did. Lana listened. Something made her turn and catch his eye. Looking at her made a strange new sensation swell in his chest: something like admiration, but prettier.

"The boys say they'll take us riding, Ron." Lana beamed. "Carlito runs his last race at six. Then we can go to their stables and the warmup track out back. They've got a swell new filly they want me to take for a trot. And the dun mare has a newborn foal I'm just aching to see. What do you say?"

"You go ahead," said Ron. "I'll get us a room. I want to lay down."

"Where shall I find you?"

"Ask your friends—what's the best hotel in town?"

She did. "Hotel Mariposa."

"Then I'm there. Find me later." On sudden impulse he kissed the top of her head. The jockeys oohed and teased and Ron swore he could see Lana's cheeks flush a pleased rose petal pink.

11

Indoor plumbing, a first in Tijuana. Ron stood under the shower spray and watched hot water shape the seaweed of his chest hair into a tributary of suds slithering down his navel. The hammering carpenter of his hangover had faded to indolent fatigue. He lingered in the shower. In the next room lazy ceiling fans circled overhead.

Mini bar bottles, green and brown like alchemic elixirs. Ron wrapped himself in a white bathrobe and twisted the cap off a vanilla extract bottle of scotch. He swallowed the drink in one smoky gulp. Smoke made him think of cigarettes and he had one too, snowy tendrils of burning tobacco curling in matador cape swirls. He flopped on the wide double bed. These bed springs, $50 a night bed springs, didn't squeak like rats but held their tongue, taciturn as priests. Siesta heat lowered his eyelids. When he awoke dusk was purple, slowly ripening to black. His cigarette was out between his fingers. Lana was not back yet.

Lana.

A hiccup in his heart at the thought of her. A power surge. *That's strange*, he thought. *Lana is a girl*. He said to himself as if explaining something delicate to a child. *Girl.* He didn't know girls. He didn't know them like he knew boys, all the planes and crannies of what lay between their thighs, what swelled and stiffened and flinched from breath and licks and touch. It felt strange to think of her in terms of the strange secret valley resting like a bird between her legs, as if imagining her lungs and heart outside her chest. But it was there, no doubt. That was what strode the saddle her thighs bounced against now, tucked inside her khaki pants like a wet little secret. A secret he had no idea how to understand.

Christ, he thought. *I don't even think I've seen pictures. Not past the triangle, at least.* He thought about her, and what she lacked, in the context of defending an imaginary war buddy. *Ol' Joe lost both arms at Normandy. That means I can make a fist when I want and he can't. But that can't stop him from being swell company. Right, Joe?*

This was more time he'd ever spent in his thirty-six years thinking about women, and the strangeness of his ruminations made him shake his head. The tiny bottles of the mini-bar twinkled like taxi dance blondes dangling unlit cigarettes. Ron jumped up and drained a gin. Juniper, ugh. It couldn't distract him from Lana.

What was it? What grabbed his thoughts like a mouse in a cat's mouth? Was it *normal?* He unscrewed the rye.

Normal. That distant horizon on every man's map, and his road always veering left. *Normal.* White picket fence. Kids. No secrets. A real wedding, one where you kissed the bride and meant it. *Normal.* The road Vera turned onto with her Navy man from San Jose. He'd told Vera, just before she left. He told her and didn't tell her, not in words but in a lingering look at the stack of movie magazines he bestowed upon her as a going away gift. He told her by daring to place shivering fingertips on the top of the stack, drawing covetous streaks of fingerprint oil slowly down Tyrone Power's face. She knew. She got it. She backed away as if he were a snake on fire, eyes big and cold like boiled eggs. *Hell's bells. You can keep your damn magazines.* Dickie Vleck never saw his best friend again.

But Lana didn't cringe or flinch or run away. He told her more of his dirt than Vera could even imagine and she said only *you poor fool*, in that soft and real contralto. She bought him a drink. They watched the races and met the jockeys. She kept his secret tucked away, so her no doubt macho friends would like him, too. Lana the brave, riding *caballos* with the rangy jockeys of Agua Caliente. Hair in the wind, tequila in her throat. He couldn't stop himself from imagining what happened next. A pebble in the track, just big enough to snag a hoof. The horse falls. Lana, thrown. The toothpick snap of her neck. Blood running out of her ears and in her gold, gold hair.

Ron sat upright. *It could happen*, he thought. Suddenly he did not want it to happen, with every fiber of his being. Suddenly he felt terribly alone. He would go and get her, now, and take her away. Drink surged his panic. He leapt from the bed and tore around the dark room, stubbing his toes and trying to remember where he put his shoes.

There was a knock at the door.

A boy, backlit against the hall light. Small, young, narrow shoulders, a jockey cap on his pert shorn head. Ron's heart clenched against bad news.

"H'lo, Ron," she said.

She stepped inside.

Lana.

Hair cut as short as a boy's.

"The jockeys did it," she said, breathless. She took off her cap and scrubbed at what was left of her hair with nervous fingers. "But just because I asked them to." She upturned her face to his in the purple dusk light, lip trembling, eyes scared and pleading in a way Ron had never seen before. He saw now the male shining through the female of her face; a boy's perfect straight nose, spray of freckles, cheekbones high like a choirboy. It plucked strings inside him.

"Do you like it?" she asked.

"Come here, you," he gasped, and grabbed her. Hugging her, kissing the top of her head. "I thought—" He couldn't let himself finish the sentence. He clutched her tight. Her beebite breasts pressed into his belly like two hard fists but he felt only her skinny shoulders, the twin axeheads of her shoulderblades shimmying under a veneer of flesh. *Like a boy's*, he thought. She hugged him back, her arms too petite to make the loop all the way around the small of his back. He felt her handprints on his back, as hot as an iron through his robe.

He lifted her chin to him. Topaz eyes, sparkling. *Boy.*

Before he stopped himself he was kissing her, parting that mouth. It was almost the same. It was softer and smaller but she sunk forward and grabbed his neck and gasped into his mouth the same way. The fire he felt wasn't fake now. He could feel her shoulders quivering underneath him. He grabbed her harder.

She wrenched free.

"I want to see how queers do it," she said, voice quavering, eyes big. "I've always wanted to know."

She walked away from him, so terrified he could see the trembling stutter in her walk. Facing away from him. Her hands at her neck, undoing the string of her peasant blouse. Linen folds opening like a white paper bag, neckline sliding around pale shoulders. She swept her bra straps off her shoulders as if embarrassed by the garment. Her fingers twisted around hurriedly to undo the clasps between her shoulderblades.

"It's good you're doing it," said Ron. "I couldn't unhook that if I tried."

She laughed, a shaky giggle. "The Lana Arleaux the audience knows is all padding," she said. Head ducked down, fingers at her waist. "The real me is . . ." She didn't finish. She tucked her thumbs into her waistband, khaki slacks sliding down her hips. She kicked the tangled slacks away from her ankles and stood there, naked, back to him, shy arms clutched to her chest. The carnival lights of the roused Tijuana strip outside throbbed red and gold on her skin, emerald and tangerine and white hot in kaleidoscopic pulses. She turned and gave him a look that made Ron's heart break. It was the look of the slave on the auction block, the one who knows whose eyes appraise and who may be found lacking. He returned as much kindness in his gaze as he could.

He could see what she meant, how her boyish figure needed foam and whalebone to fill the wardrobe department's evening gowns. Her body was light and freckled, thin-thighed and anvil shouldered like a child acrobat. In another life she would be a gamine farm girl, legs sprawled like a deer over plank fences, cartwheels in fields of endless wheat—not a silken creature made to loll on Technicolor couches and look stupidly at her leading man. She shifted her hips. Her shape changed like lights changed on her skin—ass from round to compact, juicy peach into muscled butterfly. Nothing could change the Grecian vase cinch of her waist but if he squinted her back was no less broad and breastless, her ass no less delectable than any other epicene he'd tasted. The curve of her spine in carnival light made a shadowy hollow, a languid question mark drawn in swooping charcoal above the swell of her ass. *Will you?* it seemed to ask Ron.

He walked across the room to her.

"I've always wanted to know how queers do it," she said again, as if trying to convince herself, the pitch of her voice rising with Ron's approach. "There's queers and there's me," said Ron. He put his fingertips to her shoulders and watched the now-short hairs at her nape jump like iron filings under a magnet. "You may not like what you think you want."

"Oh, I want it," she said, breathless. "I know and I do."

"I won't hurt you," he said, knowing that declaration meant one thing to him and another to her.

She didn't say anything.

He turned her around, gently, like the wind-up ballerina in a girl's jewelry box. He wanted to see. She clutched her arms to her chest, hiding her breasts in a don't-touch-me X of her elbows, but that wasn't what he needed to know. It was there, the great mystery, in a tiny bramble of true honey blonde—*so she doesn't dye her hair*, he mused, and then swallowed hard realizing that was the beginning and the end of his knowledge about girls. A novitiate humbled at the mouth of his own naivete.

He turned her around again, her back to his front, and she gasped as he clutched her around the waist in a big orangutan hold. The welcome blood surged into his groin again. This was familiar, this *pas de deux* of smaller body clutched to him, hands finding purchase at the handle of slim hipbones. How the back of the neck with its clipper-shorn hairs danced up under his nose, how the blunt buttocks filled the gap of his lap with puzzle piece perfection. The way his hardening cock found the slot of the crack of her ass without even trying. She panted in surprise and then ground against him, worrying open the slit of his robe until flesh jumped on flesh and both of them inhaled sharply. He was ready for the shock now. He was ready to feel hands closing on wrong, empty air as he reached down past her navel, through the soft tangle, to find whatever there was to find. He was braced for the what-is-it—braced for revulsion, dismay, shock and horror, whatever would rear up inside him at something so quite new. Then his fingertips touched the little pad-of-a-cat's-paw secreted in the keyhole up top, and fear melted away. It was not so terrifying. He slid two exploratory fingers down and thrilled at how her waist twisted and squirmed under his arm. Her crotch was strange and blank, true, but soft, not frightening. Awe and curiosity made him rub his finger back and forth, prodding the nub. He felt the slick of dew. Little gasps escaped from her throat. Suddenly some secret zipper parted the curtain and he was in the melting center of her pussy, plush like honey and petals but not yet swallowed inside her. He hesitated.

She read his thoughts. "You won't hurt me."

"I could."

"You won't." She took his hand, pressed his wrist down deeper between her legs. "I'll show you."

His finger trembled as she drew him closer. He made his fingers rigid—all things had to be rigid here, didn't they?—but she squeezed his hand until he relaxed and then, as softly as a glass of milk tumbling off the table's edge, he tipped inside her. It wasn't like the asshole with its tight lemon pucker, its put-em'-up fight to keep the door barred. The mouth of her cunt wanted him inside, a hostess whose greatest happiness was welcoming guests at the door. He expected a hole, a tube, a rigid ribbed hangar like the cavern Jonah found inside the whale. What he felt was an infinite pocket of crushed velvet, luxuriant and snug. *No wonder normal men get foolish chasing pussy*, he thought, delighted and surprised. *It is so nice to be inside* . . . He bent down and kissed the back of her undulating neck, chest suddenly swelling with chaste gratitude for women's burden. For the world to know you wear an open wound at all times, a thornless rose, a gate straight to your heart with no sentry . . . He pressed his finger deeper inside her and discovered a shelf of bone against his finger, a hard mountain bluff inside what was otherwise vague and soft. He pressed on the ridge and felt her body buck again inside the loop of his arm. She reared and exhaled, the flute of her throat emitting one breathy, sanctified note.

"Lots of men have been where you are," she said, breathless. "They were all different, and they were all exactly the same." She looked over her shoulder at him, shyly, pointedly. "You're not." Her voice, hushed, barely able to speak. "I don't want the same from you. "He withdrew his finger, his thumb now cresting the crack of her ass, the fingerprint of his thumb massaging the wrinkled knot tucked inside. The lunar landscape of her body now matched the terrestrial masculine map he knew once more: the clench of her buttocks, the winking divots at the base of her spine, the button of her asshole no different than any other. From behind Lana was a teenage boy, hairless and young, fresh and pliable. For one sharp unholy moment he thought about cigarettes, lit cherry tips, the ashy sizzle of flesh. It sent electricity straight through his dick but he shook off the want. *Not for you,* he promised her silently. *Not this time.*

"Come down on the bed," he whispered in her ear. She slid herself over the bedspread, legs spread like scissors, ass in the air. Hands already clenching the sheets hard. He slipped the robe off his shoulders. Carnival light painted his own body now, the two of them strange chameleons in a dense and humid jungle of their own design. He knelt behind her and whispered what he always said to virgins.

"It'll hurt."

"Please don't," she said.

Ron was taken aback. Boys never said that. Her eyes turned to his, pleading. "Please be gentle with me."

Gentle. No one had ever been gentle with him—and in turn, he'd always repaid the favor. Assumed brutality. Take it like a man. But she wasn't a man. The sight of the glistening ruby slit tucked under the crack of her ass awakened something chivalrous inside him. But the *how* of the request still stopped him in his tracks. *I'm not sure I know how,* he thought. And then, the answer unfolded inside him, like a coin dropped into a wishing well decades ago suddenly splashing *plink* at the bottom.

Do it like I wished someone had done for me.

He planted fierce kisses in the crook of her neck, licks and bites and crushing lips that made her pant hot mouthfuls of air into the sheets. Grabbing her around the waist, pulling her close, threading his cock back and forth in the crack of her ass and then the sudden inside-out shock of how he slipped inside her cunt—it was right there, wet and slippery, he didn't mean to—and how she gasped and cried out and he pumped for three stunned and seduced seconds before pulling out to her disappointed moan. She tossed her head back and bucked her hips up against him but he wouldn't relent.

"My way," he said, and she sucked her breath in between clenched teeth. He swept his robe off the floor, unthreading the terry cloth belt. "Oh my," she gasped, schoolgirl astonishment surfacing through her cultivated demeanor as he bound her wrists in tight handcuff loops—a novice's bondage, binding her not to bedposts or hooks but only to herself. She was shocked, but didn't struggle. The sight of her hands splayed over the mummy wrappings like a tree naked in autumn sent another jolt of electrified want into his cock. His cock was still slick with her juice but he had plenty of precum of his own, little gossamer drops anointing the dusky asterisk of her asshole. He could give her the full gentleman's treatment—a finger first, just to nudge her open, to get her used to that outré sensation of in, not out the out-est hole in her body. He sucked long and hard on his own index finger and looked down at her. Face down into the mattress, her skin a river of dairyland vanilla, not dulce de leche caramel, her ass only too slightly swollen to truly belong to a guy. But the resemblance was close enough to make him forget chivalry. The tip of his cock kissed her ass.

He pushed. She gasped. She shouted, out loud, the muscle of her back going rawhide hard for one shocked moment. But she didn't fight. She didn't shake him out of her. His hand on her shoulder, locking her down. This was the moment he loved, Ron reflected. When they yield. When they break. His cock was hard enough to count the tick-tock throb of his pulse, the skin so tremblingly aflame he could almost feel the tiny tick of her own pulse in the tight ring of her asshole.

He loved the whimper that rolled deep in her throat, the tremble of her lower lip, the spray of sweat that bloomed across her freckles as he plowed inside her ass.

The way the cinch of her asshole fought him, the way it convulsed and shuddered in time to the anguished bark of pleasure springing from her throat. He was only an inch inside her, only just past the corona of the ridge of his cock, and the virgin muscle choked and sputtered around him, the last spasms of pain's defeat at the altar of pleasure. "Now," she whispered, and he slid another torturous inch inside her, felt the spasm rock anew, the heavenly suction of tight ass around the tip of his cock, felt her thighs twitch beneath him as her ankles rolled in the same anticipatory figure eights he'd noticed the day he showed her his porn. He pushed harder, deeper, up to the hilt—savage now, unsparing, obeying only the sweet warm cry of *more, yes, more* that flooded his body with every push. Closing his hands around her bound wrists and thrilling to how the sparrow bones in her winding hands felt clamped in the flesh manacles of his fists.

He reached around, sinking two fingers into the pocket of her cunt. He could feel himself, feel his own cock inside her, the in and out drag of his cock fucking her ass like a loud conversation heard through a thin apartment wall.

Something broke the spell. "What are you doing?" she said, her voice rough and breathless.

He could barely catch his breath either. "You want it like queers do it," he said. "The other guy always comes."

"Not like that," she said, and took his hand, back to the nub at the keyhole. "Right here." He could feel the hard little pea of her clit underneath, a pearl tucked inside the folds of the oyster. *Girls get hard, too?* he thought with another burst of astonishment, chagrined once again by the depth of his ignorance about the fair sex. But the way her hips swung in gratified swoops at the slightest touch confirmed all he needed to know was how they were the same, not how they differed.

"What do I do?" he whispered into her ear.

"Like this," she said, and ground his finger in clumsy circles into the nub of flesh. His hand sandwiched between her body and mattress, the bone of her hip cutting into his wrist, the feverish whip of her delicate finger on top of his. Something was swirling inside her now. He could sense it in some arcane, elusive way, not in words but in sensations. Her sharp cries grew loose, ecstatic, unleashed. She was tightening now, the tourniquet of her asshole spasming around his cock in hiccupy patterns he knew well. He pushed her finger aside and smeared his hand against the slick insistent throb of her clit, aching to grab, to massage, to stroke as he knew how. His hips awakened and slammed into her again, a dot of breeze where her wet and waiting cunt kissed up against his balls. She reared back and shouted—

He came first but he felt it. He felt her body buck and her ass clench and the sound that arose from her throat seemed to originate in the *kapow* of her tightening buttocks and her slavering cunt, spiraling up through her body like a spring-loaded cannonball aimed somewhere at the stars. He came hard in her ass and still felt it, felt how different it was than his one juicy load and its exclamation point finality. She was not one jolt but many, in so many shapes: sudden hiccups and delicate twitches and hard belly dancer shimmies, coming and retreating and coming again. He flashed back to a balmy afternoon spent on some producer's patio, the ice in his julep suddenly rattling like dice in a gambler's palm. Oscars jumped off knick-knack shelves like Golden Gate suicides. The producer smiled. *San Andreas*, he said. *She's just reminding us we're all in the palm of her hand.*

"Oh God," said Lana. "You can get out of me now."

12

She lay in bed propped up on her elbows, a cigarette curled in her hand. Colored lights outside, still winking on and off in the dark like fireflies. The pink of her nipples grazed the sheets.

"What did your name used to be?" she asked.

"William Vleck. Dickie."

"Dick?" She smiled. "Prophetic."

He smiled. "Never thought of it like that." He took a drag of his own cigarette, watched the smoke curl to the ceiling. "What about you?"

"Victoria Anne-Marie Schultz. But I changed it myself, before I came to California." She took one more drag and stubbed it out on the nightstand ashtray. "I was never meant to be a Vicky."

"Or a Tori."

"Or a Schultz." She lay on her back. "Caraway bread and potato fields. And the Sunday morning smell of cornsilk tea." She dragged her fingers through her chopped hair. "I think the studio heads'll really throw me back to Bismarck now."

"I like it," he said. He rolled onto his elbow to look at her, rubbed a scrubby lock between his fingers. "You'll make them like it."

"And if I can't?"

"I'll make them."

"Big man."

"I'm your husband now." He brushed the bangs from her tomboy face. "There's things I should do for you."

She gave him a naughty smirk. "I heartily agree."

She snuggled into the crook of his armpit. The white blades of the ceiling fan spun above them, the stretched black X of its offset shadow twirling identically beneath. Black X and white blades. Black tux and white gown. Ginger and Fred, perfect partners in pirouette sync.

"Vicky and Dickie," Lana sighed. "Together at last."

13

DO TELL EXCLUSIVE—AT HOME WITH THE
DASHES! WITH 14 EXCLUSIVE COLOR PICS OF
THEIR FABULOUS HOLMBY HILLS HIDEAWAY!

Say, gals, how do you spell "love nest" in Morse code?
One thing's for sure, it's got plenty of dashes—Mr. and
Mrs. Ron Dash, that is! A great hue and cry went up
over America as millions of heartsick fans heard wedding
bells chime as blonde bombshell Lana Arleaux and hunky
heartthrob Ron Dash tied the knot on April 1st. These
April Fools are fools in love, sources say—but just how did
Lana accomplish what no other woman's been able to do—
namely, snag Tinseltown's most elusive, unmarrying-est
bachelor? What's the secret that made sparks fly between
the stars of upcoming smash hits *God Save McQueen* (him)
and *Conestoga Twilight* (her)?

"Lana understands me," says Ron candidly, as the couple lounges in the suave sitting room of their Holmby Hills mansion. "I like the company of women very much—don't get me wrong. But I'd never found one who loved the real me—the secret self I keep inside."

Ooh, sounds spooky! What's that mean, Lana—Ron's hiding the bones of some deep, dark secret he'd never let on to his millions of frothing, fainting, feminine fans? "Don't be silly," says Lana with a laugh. "It just means that Ron would prefer a quiet evening at home with a leather-bound folio of fine art to a night on the town. I'm the one who loves a lively party and the company of friends. I think that's why we're such a good match—after all, opposites attract. Ron's the steady rock, while I just love surprises."

Speaking of surprises, Lana's daring new boyish coiffure is the talk of Hollywood! "A friend cut it for me," says Lana, "I did it on a whim. You like it?" Forget about us, Lana—what'd your new hubby say when he saw his flaxen-haired bride sheared down like a sheep—and without asking for permission, even?!? "See for yourself," says this gallant Galahad. "Lana's so pretty she could wear boy's underwear to bed and I'd still be in love with her."

Above right: Ron examines physical fitness diagrams as he works out in the home gym. "The Greeks had it right," says this Greek god. "Physical health and mental health are one and the same."

Center: Ron and Lana enjoy the sumptuous ambiance of the pricey mansion they call home. "I'm lucky to be married to a man with an eye for art and furnishings," says Lana. "Ron's got such masculine good taste." And Lana's breezy cotton sundress is a little something she picked up on a recent pleasure jaunt to Tijuana. "I support native craftswomen whenever I can."

Above left: Each of the mansion's three bedrooms is done in a different bold color scheme—red, white, and dramatic black! "We don't have any one master bedroom," says Lana. "We switch rooms when we feel like it, just for fun. It's like pretending we're in a hotel without leaving home." (Take note, culture vultures—little birds tattled that the painting of the somber *señorita* hanging over the bed in the red room is just one of Ron's many wedding presents to his bride.)

Opposite: Glamourpuss Lana's quite the tiger on the red carpet—but she trades diamonds for a dishwashing apron without a thought! "I love to cook!" says this happy housewife. Hubby's favorites? Spicy Mexicali enchiladas with homemade *guacamole* (a tasty avocado spread, pounded in a traditional pestle of volcanic rock: you say it *guh-wak-a-moley*—and holy moley, is it good!)

These happy Dashes look like they've got domestic bliss all tied up in one pretty bundle . . . and speaking of bundles, Morse code operator—hear any chatter on the wire about Mom n' Pop Dash tapping out a few little Dashes? "All in good time," says Lana with a little laugh. "That's what everyone expects—and why shouldn't they? You know, Ron and I might be big Hollywood stars to the public, but at home, when the doors are closed and it's just the two of us together, we're as normal as can be."

14

"More," she panted, face down into the mattress. "I want more."

She was wearing boy's underwear, the trim band of elastic pulled down over the swell of her ass. Her hands bound to the headboard, Ron's striped red tie cutting into her wrists. The flat Kansas farmland of her back beckoned like virgin snow. The freshly lit cigarette smoldered between Ron's fingers, a perfect cylinder of ivory paper lit red at the tip like a firefly. One last shred of restraint swelled up inside him. *I can't.* The cigarette begged to differ. The cigarette felt ready to jump out of his hand.

He'd found the underwear a week before, tucked under his sweaters in the black room's bureau. Three pairs laid out like pounded veal cutlets in a cellophane pack, size S for the slimmest, boyish-est hips. The Y-yoke of the white fronts smiled at him. Y for *Yes, yes, yes.* He'd shoved it down back under his clothes, cock suddenly surging against his zipper at the thought of why she'd hid them here, in his room, not under the bras and negligees in her own bureau, in her own red room.

They'd poured on the bullshit thick for that nosy reporter—that chinless chicken of a society pages snoop in her puce matron sack dress and her quavery schoolmarm voice. Ron nearly shit a brick when he saw Darkroom Louie bringing up the rear, Speed Graphic at the ready, big flash reflector dish like a doctor's mirrored headband, ready to snoop and pry and look deep into his and Lana's tonsils. *Not today you don't*, thought Ron as he shook Louie's hand and smiled grimly. *This is my home, pal. And she's my wife. Get your dirty fingers out of her throat.*

Darkroom Louie threw him off his game. That's why he was nervous. That's why he stuttered out that horseshit about his dark secret self when the schoolmarm asked *Why Lana, my dear Mr. Dash?* Lana came to his rescue like a champ, fluttering one hand like a bullfighter distracting *el toro* while she squeezed his other hand, hard. Her touch made him grateful. As she prattled a barricade between him and the schoolmarm's questions, gratitude mellowed to a seedling of lust. He started thinking about underwear. Boy's underwear. Boy's y-front white underwear she'd bought and hid in *his* room. Not her room. Boy's underwear on her tight hips. Against her muscled ass. Pulled down around the tops of her coltish thighs. Boy's underwear, and that still-tight asshole hiding underneath—

"And you, Mr. Dash," the schoolmarm said in a fruity warble, "what do yoooooou think of your wife's stark new *hairdooooo*?"

"She could wear boy's underwear to bed," he said like a moron. Darkroom Louie suddenly got a coughing fit. Lana offered him a glass of water and shot him a look that could clean a drain. Darkroom Louie got the picture. When it came time to shoot Lana mashing alligator pears in the *molcajete*, he was minding his manners again. Lana, hunched over the pestle, pounding green creamy pulp and garlic cloves *bam bam bam*. Shaking her hips with each blow, face clenched, sweat sparkling on her brow. *Boy's underwear*, Ron thought again. He crossed his hands in front of his groin and watched her pound, transfixed. *Bam, bam, bam. Oh, oh, oh.*

Lana shut the door behind them, bidding biddie and Louie adieu with the front door's heavy *click*. "*Somber señorita on the red room wall*," she muttered to herself once they were out of earshot. She lit a cigarette, flicking out the matchhead in an aggravated snap. "She's one of those writers who likes to listen to herself being what passes for clever. Fat chance she'll go home and look up the difference between Frida Kahlo and a Juarez velvet Elvis."

Ron wasn't listening. He stared at his wife silhouetted at the door: short hair, hunched shoulders, lost angry gaze. Cigarette poised in slim fingers at her lips. Smoke curling from that perfect pert nose, like Gidget the angry dragon. He wanted her now like how iron shavings want a magnet.

"Goddamn you," he whispered.

Lana blew a megaphone of smoke from the corner of her mouth and looked at him. "Why?"

He strode across the room in three big steps, crushing her head between the big grip of his hands, lifting her face brusquely to him as if she were a cat and he needed to give her a pill. "You put them there on purpose," hissed Ron. "You bought that boy's underwear and hid it in my bedroom."

"That's men's underwear. I bought it for you."

"Liar." He spun her around and grabbed her hips, grinding his thumbs against the meat of her butt. "You know they're sniffing for blood. Any crack in the façade—"

"So what if they are?" Her face glowed satisfied with tattletale's delight. "Let them dig. We can dig faster."

Her cavalier demeanor only inflamed his outrage. "You don't get it," he hissed into her ear. "Both of us could be ruined over three little pairs of boy's underwear in my drawer upstairs—"

"Two," she said. She turned to look at him, butterscotch eyes dangerous and bright. "There's two pairs in the drawer upstairs. I'm wearing the other pair."

That broke it. Quickly he slung her over his shoulder like a caveman and pounded up the stairs, King Kong with Fay Wray in his grasp. The white room was closest. *I'm going to fuck you up*, he thought. *I'm going to make you so dirty and I'm going to do it where everything is bright and white and clean.* He threw her down on the bed and didn't let her bounce before tearing at her clothes. "Where is it?" he groaned through clenched teeth. She kicked her legs, tossing up a seafoam spray of cotton skirt as he tried to grab at her groin. "No, no, no," she giggled like a toddler, thrilled at this silly game. Ron grit his teeth. He felt his hand back up to his shoulder, a spring loaded machine that only needed one more just-try-me flash of the eyes from Lana—*yeah, just like that*—

SMACK!

The backhand caught her right above the cheekbone and threw her to the bed with a soft *whump*. "I'm not playing around," said Ron, and grabbed two clawing handfuls of her neckline. *Rrrrrip.* Thin handspun cotton tore with the sound of cracking icebergs. She wasn't wearing a bra underneath.

"Don't rip it!" she gasped. "Some poor bean farmer's wife worked *hours* to make that thing."

"I don't care," he retorted. "You want to keep your clothes, don't provoke me." He grabbed again—

SMACK!

This time it was Ron's turn for his eyes to well in horseradish disbelief. Lana scowled at him, eyes burning like the side of his slapped face, her pink nipples heaving with each angry breath through the V-shaped gash of her torn blouse. "I said *hours*," she said.

Ron grabbed her by the throat, shoved her down. "You're gonna get it now," he hissed.

"Is that a promise?" she choked out from under his grasp. His big hand framing her chin like a cameo, her teeth flashing and hungry as her bright eyes egged him on. He didn't answer her in words. He flipped her over, grabbed at the shreds of dress around her shoulders, and put his knee in the small of her back. The dress came off her back with a shriek of rending fabric , like skinning a cat. *There.* Her lithe body, denuded and shivering.

And there, just below her waist, the tight elastic of new boy's underwear gripping the hollow of her waist.

Ron fumbled at the Windsor knot at his throat and ripped the tie out from his shirt collar. He slammed her shoulders to the bed, his knees pinning her down, her legs kicking futilely behind her as he grabbed her flailing hands. "Hold still," he muttered, knowing full well she wouldn't listen. It didn't matter. The tie twisted in his hands, a well-practiced half-hitch he could do in his sleep. He slipped her hands inside the loop expertly as a rodeo rider ropes an unruly calf. In Tijuana he trusted her, binding her wrists only to each other. This time his gut told him she was going to fight. The little brat was going to squirm and wriggle and make herself slippery as a fish. Sure enough, no sooner than he'd wrapped the free end of the tie around a keyhole cutout in the headboard, she slipped one thin wrist free and tried to flip from back to front. His hand was at his belt, the jangling coin clink of the unfastening buckle. He zipped the belt out of his pant loops and slung it through the air at whipcrack speed. Flat stinging leather landed hard like snakebite against her back—

CRACK!

It scared her. She froze in disbelief and he grabbed her before she came to her senses, fastened the belt around her wrist and tied her other hand tight. Whipping didn't do it for him, not specifically, but he did like the look of the long strawberry streak rising like a sunburn across her shoulder blades. She was face down again, arms in a Y just like the yoke on the front of her boy's underwear. She yowled a smothered protest into the down coverlet.

"Shut up," said Ron, and peeled off his jacket. *The shirt stays on for now*, he thought as he rolled up his sleeves and drank in the sight of this slim-hipped creature struggling against his bonds. *Her bonds*, he corrected himself, and a little something deflated in him at the reminder. He cleared his throat, shoring up his arousal with conscious effort. *Details, details. It's not like you're going after any parts she hasn't got.* He picked up his jacket, fishing in the breast pocket for cigarettes. He didn't fall back in his groove until the flinty *kssssh* of the lighter sent another Pavlovian swell of pleasure to his tingling cock. He unzipped his fly and stroked himself absentmindedly, savoring the way her futile struggle against her bonds sweetened the kiss of fingertips on turgid flesh.

She was trying to right herself, to drag her knees up like a crawling baby and gain who knows what leverage. Ron put the lit cigarette between his lips and grabbed both of her ankles, yanking her back down to her belly with a thud.

"Uh uh," he said. "Get cute and I put you in the stocks."

"What stocks?" she spat, looking as far as she could over her shoulder. "You're bluffing."

"Maybe." He was on the bed now, kneeling between the capital A of her spread legs, his exposed cock throbbing with anticipation inches from the clean cotton underwear sheathing her ass. "Or you try me, and you find out." He folded three fingers under her waistband and pulled down. The divots over the small of her back, the way the valley of her spine melted into the voluptuous gulley of the crack of her ass. He pulled the underwear down even more and noted—not with visceral delight, but with cool, scientific satisfaction—that an egg-white strand of slick wobbled between cotton crotch and wet hungry pussy for an instant before snapping against her pink and swollen flesh.

"Just watch me," she threatened. Like a kitten hissing, trying to prickle its baby hairs to look big. The effort made Ron smile. He kept her waistband low, staring at that wet vertical smirk of a snatch. *It's just so different*, he thought, neither thrilled nor repulsed. Time and experience hadn't taught his heart to sing with angelic rapture at the sight of the thing between her legs, but he certainly didn't mind the sight of it. And wet was like hard: you couldn't fake it. Not that Lana poured on the empty flattery, but it was always nice to know when a compliment from your wife was truly, indubitably real.

"You're right," said Ron. "There's no stocks."

"I knew it," she hissed, triumphant.

"There's worse," he said. "I think you're ready now."

"Ready for wh—" she started, but he pulled the handkerchief from his jacket pocket and stuffed the gauzy wad in her mouth. She yelped and spat it out, but he knew she would. He crossed the room leisurely, listening to her spit fuzz from her tongue and curse him as he opened the closet door.

The handkerchief was a dainty rag, not nearly long enough for what he had in mind. His hand hovered above the tie rack.

"So what, another necktie?" She jerked a quick nod at the one already around her wrist. "Think that's going to scare me?"

"Chatter, chatter," he scolded. The tie went into her mouth like a horse's bit all too easily, tangling the last syllables of her protest as Ron knotted it tightly at the back of her neck. "They're right about how gabby girls are. I've never had a man talk this much in bed." The knot scrubbed against the short clipped hairs at her nape as she bucked and tossed her head—but didn't, Ron noted with some satisfaction, try to pull herself to kneeling again. She shouted something that muffled into all angry M's into the tie, a rejoinder that probably would have stung his ears if he'd heard it. The way her eyebrows bent into angry birds in flight above her watering eyes made him smile. A little cruelty went a long way when it came to making him happy.

He felt the weight of the cigarette between his lips, the way the hot cherry hovered away from his face, smoke stinging his eyes if he stood the wrong way. He sucked in a long rich mouthful and plucked the burning cigarette from his mouth, eyeing the ashy tip with some satisfaction. His eyes darted to her unmarked, unmarred back. The blood in his groin went molten, flaring up like hot coals. After a moment's contemplation, he untied the gag.

"Shhh," he said, pressing his finger to her lips. "You be good." He slid a hand down the warm patch of her underwear, finding the pearl button of her clit quickly. She inhaled sharply and ground her hips against his finger. That was one thing he'd improved in their month together, the where and why and how of her anatomy, the secret slides and compartments of the puzzle box of her cunt. Women were combination locks, not the stupid yes-no deadbolt of men's easy orgasms—but once you knew the sequence . . . Two slick fingers sliding on either side of her clit made her eyes roll back in her head. A thumb kneading at the coy folds pleated at the open end of her pussy made her mouth part in voiceless ecstasy, and the honey pouring forth slid Ron's thumb inside her without ever having to push the gatekeepers aside.

"Oh," she gasped, carnal euphoria stripping her vocabulary bare. She shut her eyes, ground hard against his hand. "Oh." She was tightening now, the pulse thrumming in the hard knot against her pussy wall, little butterfly flutter spasms flickering in the muscle like sparks on wool sweaters on crisp autumn afternoons. She wasn't close, but she wasn't far, either. He could switch two fingers for his thumb, nudge that knot hard and fast until her hips rode up in the air and she was speaking the faith healer tongues of a woman riding close to the ultimate. He could make her come now just by touching her. He'd done it before, so many times. It was just like tying a knot—the first three are clumsy, the next three are practiced, the next thirty quick and sleek and tight. Glance her clit with the meat of her thumb, just as she's got her cunt deep around your fingers as it'll go. Let her swoon and gasp, pounding hard, rubbing fast, swirling around that bullseye, that jackpot, that luscious payday, and then go in for the kill as she suddenly explodes like Fourth of July. He could do it. It would be easy.

He took his hand away.

A strangled cry escaped her throat. "More," she panted, face down into the mattress, sharp disappointment twisting her voice to a heartbroken, wounded dog whine. "I want more."

He said nothing. He stood above her, watched her pant, watched her buttocks heave and her back undulate in erotic torment. He unbuttoned his shirt and slid his pants down past his cock. She was crying now, true angry tears staining hot spatters into the comforter. He took the cigarette from his mouth and held the fiery tip over her back like a dart. He could almost smell the sizzle of the fine white baby hairs scattered over her skin. He was so hard now, his cock poised up against her asshole like a battering ram. She felt it there. She bucked. She wriggled. Eager and scared. He held the cigarette inches from her flesh and relished the moment just before he knew he would do it.

"Oh god," he said, and let the hammer down.

Tsssssss.

She screamed. "Jesus Christ!" she yelled. "What did you do?" Quick, his cock squeezing into her, shutting her up with a howl and a moan and the mortar and pestle *bam bam bam* of his hard hips against her ass, his cock sliding taffy-thick strokes in and out of her. It didn't look like much, the perfect little birthmark of a burn just inside the crook of her neck, but the sight of that scabby red dot did something voltaic to him. He was ready to burn her again again but he looked down, saw the glimpse of boy's underwear tangling under his balls, her ass, the dot—it was all too much and he came in a sudden, *show's over folks* geyser.

He pulled out of her, flopped next to her, panted, head abuzz with lingering pleasure. She lifted her head.

"What the hell . . . ?" She tried to see the burn at the back of her neck, as impossible a task as kissing her elbow. "What did you . . . holy fuck, you didn't." She grimaced. "You didn't burn me with that cigarette . . . did you?"

The disbelief in her voice made him sit up. He watched her strain to see what he'd done, brows knotted in shock. *She didn't ask for that*, he realized with a crushing pang of guilt.

"I thought you knew that was coming," he said feebly.

"Knew? Jesus, Ron, I can't guess a crazy thing like that."

"But you read the article about me, and Grayson T—" A second, sharper stab of guilt cut through him. *How stupid. It wasn't her. It was the busboy. Flaco. He was the one who said he knew how much I liked cigarettes. Who said he wouldn't mind if I burned him.* He pressed his fingertips to his eyes, too ashamed to look at the woman still bound and spread-eagled next to him on the bed. *Oh God, kill me now.*

"I'm so sorry," said Ron. He grabbed at her restraints and untangled them, scooping up her tiny body in his arms, cradling her like a baby against his chest. "I won't ever, ever do that again."

"It hurts."

"I'll fix it." He carried her to the bathroom, set her down gently on the toilet. He wet a cotton ball with red Mercurochrome and dabbed at the burn. She winced at the first touch but let him minister to her.

"Jesus, Ron," she said. Her eyes focused hard on the tile floor. "I really try, you know?"

He stopped, cotton ball hovering in midair like a bloody cloud.

"What do you mean, you try?"

"I mean . . ." She snapped the underwear's waistband, as if the slap of elastic on skin explained better than words. "I know this can't be fun for you. So I try. I cut my hair. I wear the things you like. I let you . . ." She trailed off, then bit her tongue and took a breath. "No, that's not right. I don't *let* you fuck me up the ass. I *want* you to. So I do all the other things because I know . . ." She trailed off again, this time letting the open end of her sentence die against the cool bathroom tile.

Ron picked up the tail of her discarded thought. "Because you know I'd rather be doing it to a boy." *Ouch. Kinder truths have killed*, he thought, regretting his candor instantly.

"Yeah," she said. She looked at him. "And all I ask is that you don't burn me with cigarettes."

"Done," he said, dropping to his knees and taking her hands in his. "Never, never, never again." He knew he meant it when he said it, because something immolated to ash inside him, a little crushed out puff of tobacco shreds, cold and dead.

15

Usually they slept in separate rooms—that "switching rooms" jive was all hooey, good copy spun for that pesky reporter—but tonight he lay beside her in the red room. *Her* room. John the Baptist on the floor, green glass eyes glittering, mouth open in perpetual, accusatory snarl. Ron's inner self-reproach, made incarnate as décor.

He turned to look at her. She was laying on her side away from him, the sharp tomboy planes of her back peeking out over the top of a plain cotton nightie. A protective hand covered the scar he'd blotted onto the corner of her neck. Shielding the wound but still laying beside him. The contradiction made his heart ache with pity.

Make it up to her, he thought.

"Lana," he murmured, brushing her skin with the back of his fingertips. She stirred but didn't quite awaken. He spooned his body around hers, the curve of his body so big it threatened to swallow her, like an egg tucked in a grapefruit rind.

Wrapping his arms around her waist, kissing the unscarred side of the crook of her neck, blank and unviolated. She sighed, surfacing out of dreams. He pressed his face to the back of her head and waited, blinking butterfly kisses on the short scrubby crop of her hair until she roused and turned to face him. In the dark all he could see of her hazel eyes was the glitter of light on their liquid surface, and how when she blinked the glint lifted and settled, like ripples on dark water. She stared at him, waiting.

He didn't dare kiss her face. *Not after what I've done*, he thought. *I've lost the privilege*. He kissed the crown of her head and bent down, pushing back red velvet sheets to crawl low under the covers. She squirmed and pulled the hem of her baby doll nightie tight over her tense thighs. He lay his hand gently on hers. "I won't," he said, and she relaxed, just a little. His heart thrummed in his chest and on a whim he took one of her hands and laid it on his sternum, on the stain of dark hair between his nipples. "Can't you feel it?" he said, voice suddenly shy.

She shook her head.

"My heart," he said. "I'm scared."

"Of me?"

He didn't answer. It was the truth. He lowered his head and kissed the back of her hand. *So different than a man's hands*, he thought. Slim and narrow and the short fingers stood almost all the same height, like a cluster of ladies-in-waiting. He could not pretend they were a man's, and he could not pretend they were a boy's, even with the naked and unlacquered nails she preferred to the burgundy talons starlets wore *de riguer*. The knuckles didn't knob and the tendons twitching in the back were fine like bird's bones. They were a woman's hands. They were hers. "Lana Arleaux," he whispered, kissing them again. "Lana Arleaux's hands."

The incantation gave him courage. He slid on top of her and named the landscape. "Lana Arleaux's face," he said, trembling fingers fumbling to unbutton the top of her nightie. "Lana Arleaux's neck and shoulders and collarbone." She raised her hands to help him but he shook his head. He would do this by himself or not at all. He parted the thin rayon and swallowed hard. Lana Arleaux's breasts, nipples so pale pink the aureole disappeared in the dark. All he could see was the gumdrop shadows of her nipples, upright in chill air or excitement or both.

He could not pretend this time. He could not pretend this was a boy's body beneath him. He forced himself to notice the differences, not the common ground. The smooth shaved armpits and the swan neck. The swoop of her waist into widening hips. The deep shot glass of her navel, sunken into the silk pillow of her belly, and the gold triangle of fur beneath. He put his quavering hands on her breasts. *Soft*, he realized with a little sunbeam of surprise. He thought breasts would be hard, buttock-solid things that needed the heavy artillery of nosecone brassieres to lock them in place. Not at all—they were fragile and tender, more like water than earth. She was not busty, but what she had yielded soft and warm and heavy under his palms. He palmed and kneaded her breasts and she sighed, undulating her back in catlike gratitude. "Nipples," she whispered, and he placed his thumbs on the fat nubs—god, one more thing so different than a man's—and a trill escaped her throat.

On an impulse he went to kiss her but stopped himself in time, planting his lips instead on the flat acre between her breasts. She didn't flinch. His palms, still caressing her nipples, his lips kissing down, down, down, his kisses springing first against underlying bone and then yielding against the plush meadow between sternum and cunt. He lingered in the gully of her navel for a moment, breathed in, flicked his tongue against it, found with some surprise that the soft nook etched in her belly could swallow the tip of his tongue. She wriggled. "Tickles," she whispered, and Ron caught the glint of smiling teeth. It gave him courage to kiss down further. His fingers kneaded the insides of her thighs nervously. He had seen it and touched it but there was one thing he'd never done, and the sanctity of it scared him to death.

But he owed her. And he *owed* her, not just in the contract of mutual pleasure but the contract of their marriage. He was married to a better friend than he'd ever found in any of the lithe young men who'd stained his bedsheets. Except this friend was a woman, fifty-nine inches and ninety-eight pounds of everything different. *Now or never*, he thought. He bent his head and lapped a tentative lick at the keystone arch where her clit tucked into the bramble. She shivered and he jumped back in alarm.

"It's okay." Her hand on his shoulder, the black marbles of her eyes shining courage in the dark. "You don't have to—"

"I want to." He licked again, this time longer and deeper. The tang of lemon, like a battery touched to the tongue to test its voltage. He smiled, surprised. Boys tasted bitter and sweet but girls were sour and salty, the strange symmetry of sexual flavor. He licked his lips and tried again, this time straining to sense with his tongue the pearly knot of her hardening clit under the silk kimono folds of the flower of her cunt. It was there—*she* was there—slippery, molten, proud like a shiny new marble. He found it between his teeth and his lips and his tongue, sucking and nudging and milking its essence loose. She groaned and dug her nails into his shoulder.

Absurd delight suddenly burbled up inside him. He'd heard about how girls take a long time. The first time he went at her with his fingers he was braced for muscle cramps but to his surprise she came so quickly. The next time was even quicker, and the third he had to show some restraint to draw out the climax and give her her money's worth. He saw now that frigid women were casualties of clumsy partners, the kind of amateurs that blame their tools instead of their technique. Women weren't a mystery. The mystery was why most men didn't care. Why? Were they helpless against the *now now now* nag of their own penetrating need, lashed to the mast of their own cocks like Odysseus swooning after the Sirens? He wasn't like that, not with her. Was his own lukewarm regard for the female form the key to plucking the moon from the sky and handing it to her on a silver platter?

She shifted, rolling over onto her stomach in a fairy breath rustle of bedsheets. He stopped her, gently. "This way," he said, hands on the tops of her shoulders, pressing her down onto her back, the significance of his words nearly bursting inside him like overpuffed balloons.

She clasped her hands gently behind his neck, pressed her forehead to his. "It's okay," she said in a whisper, the volcano assuring the virgin sacrifice soon to swim in the lava below.

Everything in the room grew sharp and articulate, the edges of dressers and tables and chairs suddenly razor-true in panic, like lines on a blueprint. Ron squinched his eyes tight, barely daring to look at the woman beneath him. He'd been inside her before, for those three strange seconds in the hotel room, but the heat of that moment was fanned by all the lust for young boys he'd projected on her. To shut off the projector, to pay attention to only the girlish flesh beneath him suddenly filled him with deer-in-headlights panic. He would have to do it by feel. He was too terrified to do any other way. He hesitated so long she finally took pity on him and wriggled her hips beneath him. Her cunt kissed his cock, anointed it with a hot dab of dew, nudged and caressed it until it was easier to push than it was to resist. Instantly he was balls deep in comfortable velvet and didn't regret his decision at all.

"Oh god," she mouthed softly but he barely heard. He was concentrating hard, forcing his attention to how the marrow of her felt different this time as he slid in and out, as how his hips knocked against the open gate of her inner thighs instead of the pillow of her ass. The difference was subtle but true, and he liked it. He ran his hands over her breasts, tweaked the nipples, pawed, squeezed, listened to her pant and whimper and hiss in reply to his touch. It was not bad. It was pleasant. It was something he could do with relish, not duty, not just tonight but always. This was his ticket to normal. *Normal.* It all swam before him in a halcyon haze. Domesticity. The key unlocked, the entrance finally his. Leave behind the boys and the cigarette burns and all your clinging sickness and here is normal. Sliding inside her cunt felt as satisfyingly masculine as piloting a shiny new Cadillac up the suburban driveway. Wife and kids cheering him on, dog cavorting at a little boy's feet. Husband, provider. Man in the grey flannel suit. Clean laundry billowing on a backyard clothesline. Sunny days as rose-scented as a Douglas Sirk montage. Thoughts of the Mexican rose up and he pushed them down like drowning a kitten. Push inside her, pull out. Not so different after all. Everything is okay. The mantra rocked back and forth in his head with the pulse of his hips. She is here. She is lovely. He kissed her and she kissed back, lips teasing, biting, her kisses hot with exhalations. *Everything is okay. Everything is okay. Every—*

"Hhhh . . ." he sputtered, and came in spite of himself. Lana gasped and clutched the back of his neck and it was over. Sealed. Consummated. They'd done plenty in bed, sure, but try telling that to the judge. He felt annulments slipping away. He felt Rockwell applauding the slugger, like fathers do at Little League games. *Well done, my son.*

121

She coughed and shifted under the sheets, away from him. He did the same, laying beside her, his heartbeat gently decrescendoing into tranquility

"Do you ever think about that Mexican?" she said.

A jab of adrenaline skyrocketed his pulse for a moment. Ron almost asked *Who?*, the reflexive lie of the habitually cautious. But he bit his tongue and instead dredged up the truth from some ocean floor inside himself.

"All the time."

"When you're with me?"

"Yes."

"When you're fucking me?"

"Yes." He shifted on his elbow. "But not this time."

"I know." She looked at him, topaz eyes bright. "I could tell."

She tucked her head closer to his chest and he curled his arms around her. They said nothing to each other. Nothing ticked into minutes of silence. His limbs grew heavy and somnolent and his breathing slowed to the same meditative pace as the woman laying beside him. John the Baptist's eyes gleamed bright and watchful into the night.

Just before winking out he felt something leave his body. Ethereal and androgenated, slipping out through his ribs with a heartplucking twinge. White jacket and nosebleed and cinnamon bun. Blue eyes and *dulce de leche*. One last vibrato twang of agonizing, grief-stricken loss and then it left. He felt the ache of the vacancy in his heart for one wretched raw moment before picket fences and blue skies sucked in and packed the void. *That's the past*, he thought.

Here's my future. He took one last deep breath and sank into sleep like a skindiver parting the void.

16

Los Angeles, 1958

He saw the twin billboards on the drive to Rockwell's office. Him and Lana, their portraits side by side. RON DASH is CLIVE MCQUEEN in GOD SAVE MCQUEEN. Ron's doppelganger, gun in hand, tall enough to ride the H of the HOLLYWOOD sign like a hobby horse. And next to him, in blue bonnet and calico pinafore, LANA ARLEAUX in CONESTOGA TWILIGHT. Paintbox sunset, wagon wheels, Injuns lurking behind saguaros, his wife blonde and noble in the unforgiving Badlands. *No cacti in South Dakota*, Ron thought with a smirk. *That's the Tinseltown magic machine for you.* On any day but today it would have ruined his mood. Not today. Things were good today. Even dumb billboards unworthy of his beautiful wife were worth enjoying.

The studio shipped her out to Arizona last June. He'd fucked her good that final month, learned how to make her teeth chatter and her body convulse with remorseless, jactitating pleasure, watched that gratified shameless smile break out underneath her closed eyes, that feels-so-good row of gleaming white teeth he'd learned to crave more than his own climax. He never tied her up, never let her offer the apricot of her ass to his eager cock ever again. She shipped off to Nogales with a kiss and a smile and in her absence Ron made himself busy.

They welcomed him back at Ultimate, where Eddie at the front kiosk waved him in again and execs didn't mind sharing a table with him at the commissary. He spent mornings dubbing *Hammer Of Fate* and the afternoons in wardrobe tests, handgun experts, Cockney dialect coaches. At night he sank into the script Rockwell couriered over to the house. He memorized superspy Clive McQueen's lines backwards and forwards, retreating to the basement gym in the dark hours and huffing out rejoinders to long-lashed double agents and ultimatums to fiendish Oriental masterminds in between bench presses and chin ups, pressing reps until sparkly confetti swam at the corner of his vision. He slept hard.

When the studio needed nothing from him he attacked the house with do-it-yourself ferocity. The sunroom needed painting. He poured a whole crew's worth of effort into the Zen demands of the task—spread dropcloths, tape off edges, pour buttermilk paint into a battered tray, stroke the roller back and forth with monasterial calm. He nailed wobbly baseboards and retightened screws and mowed the lawn himself, sweating every vegetal acre behind a creaky push mower. When that restless, unutterable itch surfaced even under that kind of distraction he downed a scotch and drove to Art DuPuis's on Rodeo Drive. Time to buy some jewelry.

Monsieur DuPuis was suave gray, pewter hair slicked back like a swain and suit the same soft taupe as a mourning dove. He watched patiently as Ron scrutinized the baubles laid out on black velvet before him. They were all lovely. Soapy dots of chalcedony, virescent emeralds, moonstones and lapis and amethyst strung into bracelets and ringed with gold soft and pure enough to wear a skeptic's bite marks. Indecision knotted Ron's brow.

"Dear Miss Carol," called DuPuis to the ginger-haired shopgirl up front. "Would you be so kind as to lend us your wrist?" The girl took one look at Ron Dash and couldn't hide a gulp of delight but stood as patiently as a petting zoo pony as DuPuis clasped a bracelet of black and white pearls around her willing wrist. She twisted her arm here and there, letting Ron watch the caviar of beads spill and dangle against her pale skin.

DuPuis noticed Ron's frown. "Perhaps you've an inspiration about improving the piece?"

"Black, white—and red," said Ron. "Those colors have . . . *sentimental* meaning for us."

"There's open links for extra jewels." DuPuis swept a finger along the bracelet's fat chain. "I've some lovely pigeon's blood rubies. Direct from Burma. My gemcutter will weep to carve them up but I'll make it so for you."

Ron thanked the man and paid cash, a thick stack of two weeks' salary.

"Return in a week," said Monsieur DuPuis. "I'll have it ready by then."

Lana sent a telegram. NOGALES AZ JUN 13 DEAR MR MCQUEEN AM HAVING A PERFECTLY DREADFUL TIME IN THE DESERT STOP SICK AS A DOG WITH CHUCK WAGON CHOW AND READY TO FAINT MOST 103 DEGREE DAYS STOP DONT COME RESCUE ME THE INJUNS WILL GET YOU STOP ILL WRAP THIS SORRY SPECTACLE UP AS SOON AS I CAN AND COME HOME TO YOU STOP LOVE LANA PS I TOLD THE GRAND CANYON ABOUT YOU AND NOW SHES JEALOUS

The telegram burned in his hands. He'd awaken at dawn, down raw eggs and a bennie, sweat out last night's guilty dreams before heading to the studio. He'd squeeze a spring hand grip in the makeup chair and shout out the crossword to the script girl before being called to the set. Anything to keep your mind off what you're not supposed to be thinking about.

That night he figured it's not cheating if you think about your wife while you do it. Cock in hand, sweating nervous beads of vodka through his pores, thoughts darting to that fat file secreted in his bedroom, like how you can't keep your tongue off a new gold tooth. He'd come so quickly if only he could see those boys, the jockstraps pulled down to the root of half-hard cocks, the ribsy fingers of muscle garnishing their nipples like angel wings. In a seizure of self-righteousness he thundered to his feet and stormed into his room, cock leading the way like a dowsing rod.

Trembling hands could barely fit the key into the lock and when he grabbed the accordion file it upended in his hands like a cat escaping a bath. A fluttering rain of glossy photos spilled hard on the floor, an assembled forum of hungry mouths and cocks and assholes stretching out like a chiaroscuro carpet. The ghosts of past phantom lovers, returning in one last haunting. *Sure you want to do this, Ronnie dear?* He scooped them up in frantic arms, refusing to look at them as he hurried down the stairs to the maw of the fireplace. He threw them on the logs and struck a match. The poisonous vinegar smoke of burning photos, choking and purifying like holy incense, filled the room as a hundred boys went up in flames.

He returned to DuPuis. The bracelet was there, resplendent in a grey velvet box. "What else do you have?" said Ron, and the ginger haired shopgirl joined them once more. DuPuis dangled pale blue sapphire teardrops from her ears. Ron winced.

"Earrings are so close to the face," he said. "No offense, miss, but it's hard to judge when she's not the woman wearing them."

"I understand," said DuPuis. He raised one elegant eyebrow. "Perhaps Madame has a favorite motif that would make a striking brooch?"

Ron returned a week later for Lana's red star, a solid pentagram set with garnets. *Not quite the kind of goods the workers unite for*, he thought as he signed the sizable bill. *But it's the thought that counts.*

"A star for a star," DuPuis smiled. "And perhaps Madame has a favorite flower?" Ron returned for an ivory cigarette case, daisies carved in cameo, the nubbly center of each blossom dotted with citrine rhinestones the color of sunny champagne.

"And what color are Madame's eyes?" This time Ron bought her three tawny rings, thick stacking bands of gold set with warm octagons of topaz. "Please have these sent to her trailer, in Arizona," he informed DuPuis, and headed out the door.

At home there was another telegram waiting.

NOGALES AZ JUL 22 RON PLEASE ARRANGE LONG DISTANCE CALL TO STUDIO WAGON NOGALES 3-4558 IS URGENT BUT NOT DIRE STOP LOVE YOU DARLING LETS TALK SOON

He dialed.

"Ron," she purred.

She told him.

"But don't tell them," she said, voice quavering. "I've still got the big wagon chase scene."

"They can't make you do it," said Ron, ire rising. "I won't stand for it. Come home."

"I'm all right. I want to finish. I've only got eighteen days more on location."

"That's eighteen too many. You tell that know-it-all Wyler he'd better get your trailer air-conditioned and quick. If he doesn't I'll drive down there myself and beat the stuffing—"

"Ron," she said, her voice as soft and close as her hand on his arms. "I'll be all right."

He swallowed hard.

"I'm tough stuff," she said, her little girl voice sharpening her words into truth. "We both are."

He returned to the store the next day.

"Have you sent the rings?" he demanded to DuPuis.

"Yes, sir, by armored courier. They should arrive—"

"Recall them," he interrupted. "I want something else. I want the most beautiful stone you have, in this store or in your safe or anywhere at all."

DuPuis nodded with the gravity of a chancellor. "Dear Miss Carol," he said to the shopgirl. "Please lock the front door and draw the shades." She nodded, face solemn, and produced a jangling garland of keys as DuPuis soundlessly disappeared into the back. Ron waited, fidgeting, drumming fingers on the glass countertop. One shade at a time came down, darkening the room like a midday eclipse.

DuPuis returned, stepping into the center of the jeweler's light like an emcee mounting the stage. In his hands he held a wide flat book of a velvet case. He placed it on the countertop with the gravity of an ancestor's bible and undid the clasp. Ron's breath caught in his throat.

The biggest gem he'd ever seen, so flawless and huge his untrained eye assumed it was a scarlet wedge of stained glass. Cut in a noble, perfect triangle, mounted with six talon-like prongs at the throat of a delicate choker mounted with hundreds of stardust diamonds. He swallowed hard.

"Another ruby?" he asked.

"A diamond. Red is the rarest color, true reds like this rarest of all. This is the Hubbard-Danahy Diamond. Trilliant cut, twenty-seven carats. Colored stones have descriptive grades that are, I think, quite poetic. This stone's grade is Fancy Vivid. That sounds perhaps like Madame," he said with a wink.

"Where did you find this?"

"Usually a stone such as this is sold at auction with a great deal of fanfare. Speaking candidly, I find the process vulgar." He sniffed. "I am pleased that my reputation has allowed this stone to come into my care whilst still preserving her honor. It has changed many hands but I assure you that it is not cursed. Miss Carol?" The shopgirl came over, trembling.

DuPuis looked at Ron. "I must ask your permission to place this stone upon a woman other than your intended."

"Please," said Ron, and DuPuis lowered the necklace over the shopgirl's neck like donning a horse with a bridle.

"Why—it's cold!" the shopgirl burbled in spite of herself as DuPuis fastened the multiple clasps, an astonished hand flying to the wine-colored bauble now hovering in the notch of her collarbone. DuPuis nodded indulgently, a man used to seeing women gush nonsense in the presence of a formidable gem.

"We can change the mount if you desire," said DuPuis, gesturing to the stone around her throat. "Some women feel confined by a choker."

"That won't be necessary," said Ron. "I'll take it."

"Very good, sir. Armored courier?"

"The fastest," said Ron. "And I'd like to include a note."

DuPuis produced a creamy stack of embossed stationary. "At your leisure," he said, gesturing to an antique correspondence desk in the corner.

The words swirled out of the pen in a delirium of happiness.

> *Dear Lana,*
> *Not nearly a fair trade,*
> *but I hope this necklace makes you just as happy*
> *as you and baby have made me.*
> *You make a beautiful mother,*
> *Love,*
> *Ron.*

Two days later: NOGALES AZ AUG 01 GOLLY MISTER STOP FOR A ROCK LIKE THAT I'D HAVE LET YOU KNOCK ME UP MONTHS AGO

17

Ron still carried the folded telegram in his breast pocket as he parked in the garage outside Rockwell's office. It really was all too good, sometimes. Not long ago—almost one year, wasn't it? *Good God,* he thought, *one short year.* Last February the only choice he needed to make was whether to drink himself to death slowly or quickly. Now a respectable future was unfurling itself more grandly than any red carpet ever did.

Rockwell greeted him with a back-slapping handshake. "Clive McQueen, secret agent. Victor Bernstein at Ultimate says *God Save McQueen's* testing better in previews than anything else this year. They're sticking with the Valentine's Day release. Domesticity becomes you, Ron." He clasped his hand in his with the pride of a father-in-law. "You're looking well."

"Thank you."

"How's Lana?"

"Also well. I'm picking her up at the doctor's this afternoon."

"Nothing serious, I hope. Drink?" He crossed the room, uncorked a lead crystal carafe with a *clink*.

Ron shook his head. "Just routine. I even know what he'll say to her: keep your weight down and stop wearing high heels."

"And don't reach for things over your head. Problem is, at her altitude, *everything's* over *her* head. 'Go-get-it-dear' Dash, that's how we'll bill you from now on." He clapped Ron on the shoulder. "In all seriousness, Ron . . . I'm very glad for both of you."

"Thank you."

"And I know *you* must be happy, too. Because when I see your name in the paper," he smiled wryly, "I don't reach for the nitroglycerin tabs anymore."

Ron gave a good-natured laugh. "Marriage suits me," he said, sinking into a chair. "I should have tried it sooner."

"Here's where I say 'I told you so.'" The intercom on Rockwell's desk buzzed. He tapped the heavy button. "Send him in," he said before the secretary could speak. "And since you've been behaving yourself, Ron," said Rockwell, crossing the room, "things have been good on my end, too. All the Dale DeVance worries are in the past. I'm recruiting now. Hiring."

"I know what that means."

"Let's not be crass. I'm in the business of new faces. And I've found a doozy this time." The doorknob turned, the door opening a tentative crack.

Ron suddenly flashed back to Iowa, the blond kid, the motel, the set-up. Just when everything was going well, just when he'd allowed himself to be happy about Lana and her pregnancy, Rockwell couldn't leave well enough alone. He had to rub Ron's face in how he controlled him, every aspect of his life, right down to whom he slept with. *Incest, the game the whole family can play*, Ron thought bitterly. He didn't want to meet Iowa. Not after he'd spilled his secret about the Mexican, about how lost he was, about how if he could he'd undo this whole sorry debacle—

Rockwell waved encouragement to the unseen mystery guest. "Come on in, son. Ron, I'd like you to meet the newest member of Rockwell Talent." Ron turned to face the young man entering the room, and suddenly felt like he'd been punched in the gut.

It was him. *Him.* It was blue eyes and *dulce de leche* skin and *ay dios mio.* He was no longer dressed in elevator boy whites but in a sleekly tailored single-breasted suit and stovepipe pants. His Brylcreemed hair was now squared on his head in sensuous chocolate waves. Rockwell had groomed him, shaped him, scrubbed off all the wetback and trimmed him into All-American topiary, a fresh canapé on the teen market hors d'oeuvres tray. But Ron could tell.

Flaco Sandoval. *Him.*

The boy's lips parted a little in half-concealed delight when he saw Ron. Ron gulped. He saw now where he'd broken the bridge of the boy's nose, and how the lump had been partly reset by pricey surgeons. A profile that was once too girlish and porcelain now had a subtle, rugged

18

The obstetrician's waiting room was full of pregnant women, all of them swollen in gaily printed maternity smocks like roly-poly Easter eggs. When Ron entered all their eyes turned to him, a little gasp rippling through the room underneath the ruffling sound of magazine pages. Ron felt the temperature of the room go up half a degree, a dozen hormonal incubators suddenly aflutter, burning calories at the sight and scent of a real live movie star. Ron smiled as sincerely as his tortured heart allowed.

The sight of that beautiful boy's face had ripped through Ron like a spit rod skewering a suckling pig. He shook hands with "Pace Hammond" as the edges of the room wobbled. He smiled and nodded when Pace and Rockwell nodded at him. He didn't mirror the sparkle of recognition in the boy's eyes, or the guileless way Flaco's face collapsed in disappointment when Ron didn't—*wouldn't*—acknowledge this wasn't their first meeting.

Flaco bit his tongue as Rockwell sang his praises as a star pupil of the patented Rockwell Agency starmaking process, how motivated, how gifted, how willing to learn —"A real animal intelligence, this one." Ron had that drink after all, gulping down warm scotch and trying so hard not to think about the hotel room, rumpled sheets, the buoyant ass grinding against his cock. Flaco was thinking it too. Ron could tell as clearly as a cat knows it's going to rain, the electric crackle in the air setting its fur ashiver.

Lana stepped out of the office wearing her usual nipped-in suit, an extra gusset tailored at the waist for the little lump of heir swelling beneath her top button. The sight of her chic, unmatronly attire sent a bolt of annoyance through Ron. *Why can't she wear proper mother-to-be clothes like everyone else in the room?* he thought. *It's indecent.*

"She's doing very well, Mr. Dash," said the obstetrician. "See if you can't break her of wearing those high heels."

Ron smiled, the conundrum swirling in his head. *I can't let Rockwell ruin that beautiful boy. But maybe I've already ruined him. So it's my responsibility to save him. But if I save him I can't have him. And, oh dear god, I want him. But I can't have him and keep this comfortable life that's nothing but one big lie. Well, except Lana. Lana's not a lie. And neither is the baby. Oh god, the baby.* He gave a distracted nod to the overheated women in the lobby and walked out, Lana leaning on his arm.

"He's right about those heels," said Ron. "You're going to pitch forward like a drinking bird."

"Pssh. I've been wearing high heels since I was fifteen years old," she demurred. "They're ankle strap. I'll be fine."

"They're not necessary."

"I have a short body and a tall soul. So yes they are. Besides, I hate doctor's offices. They're just one stack of well-thumbed magazines away from being a hospital." She shuddered. "Allow me my lucky totems. I need them."

He opened the car door for her, his mind still churning over the afternoon's meeting. *Ron here just signed a deal at Ultimate, same as you. Pace.* She tucked herself into the front seat of the car in one rolling motion, like a ship docking. *In fact, he'll be on soundstage A-17 while you're shooting the B-picture on A-18, am I right?* Her hair was growing out, the fringy tips of a pert blonde pageboy skimming under her beret. Rockwell's wink: *You boys can keep an eye on each other.* She plucked a cigarette from the daisy case while Ron rounded the car and sank into the driver's seat.

"That doctor's so stupid," said Lana, snapping out her lighter. "I should go to Mexico to have this baby. The women there don't get scolded if they sit on cold cement steps. Oh, look at this," she whined. There was a cigarette burn in the dashboard, a little umber navel of singed plastic. "When did this happen?" She dabbed at the dot scarred into the vinyl with her middle finger. "Did I do that?" She clucked her tongue in self-reproach. "Damn me, you just got this car too—"

"It's not you," Ron snapped. "Don't pick at it, you'll make it worse."

"But how—"

"I did it. I dropped a lit cigarette. The dealership will fix it." He didn't tell her he'd done it on purpose, in the garage, alone, after the meeting. Pretending the brown vinyl was the boy's skin. Burning a hole in his brand new car while frantically jerking away the hard-on he couldn't take with him into an obstetrician's office.

If she caught the warning in his tone she paid no mind. "The studio won't let me work on that new movie," she said, changing the subject. "That new song and dance pic. *Tango To Tangiers* or some such nonsense."

"I thought you didn't want to work on it."

"I didn't at first. Not with Sean McKelly, that slave driver of a choreographer. But I'd like the money. And I'm tough enough."

Annoyance was roiling into anger inside him. "You're due the last week of February. Rehearsals start after St. Patrick's Day."

"So what? Sean will be hungover and I'll be just out of confinement. We'll be handicapped exactly the same." She sighed. "God, I can't wait to get blotto again. I can't wait to dance again. I'm so sick of being treated like an invalid. Don't drink too much. Don't exert yourself. Don't gain too much weight or I'll put you on diet pills." She ran a hand over her sizeable belly. "Everyone's got to put their two cents in on me and Kewpie." She turned to him. "Ron, why are we still here? We could be in Mexico right now. Or Cuba. I've seen pregnant women scrubbing floors and herding pigs in Tijuana. No one treats them like they've got a disease."

"I don't speak Spanish."

"You could learn. We could ditch this crazy town, raise our baby somewhere where people are decent."

"With Castro as a godfather?"

"Maybe." She shuddered. "God, Dr. Hanley says he's going to knock me out with ether whether I want it or not. And I don't want it. You know, in Mexico, they don't knock you out when you go to deliver. They've got traveling midwives. You can have the baby right there in your own bed and when they're done—"

"Jesus, Lana!" Anger jumped into his hands, anger yanking the steering wheel and sending them almost headlight to headlight with a turquoise DeSoto in the opposite lane, the other driver's eyes big and white for one frozen moment before Ron came to his senses and careened the car back onto the road. The tires screeched and slid, thundering on to the grassy shoulder, flat rubber flapping *pathudda pathudda pathudda* on one naked rim until they rolled to a stop.

Lana panted, clutching the dashboard with both hands. Ron stared at her, eyes hard, rage boiling in his gut. "Goddammit, don't you dare think about endangering our baby like that."

"Jesus, Ron—" Lana's face was white with shock, one hand still pressing against the dashboard like a girl defending herself from a fresh date. "What's gotten into you?"

"Why do you have to be like this?" he sputtered. "Why are you so goddamn *contrary*? A million women in America are thrilled to have their babies in a clean, well-lighted hospital with a *doctor* in attendance. But oh, no that's not good enough for you. You'd rather . . . "—he struggled to spit out the coarse image—"you'd rather squat over a dirt

143

floor underneath a framed picture of Lenin just to prove some cockamamie point. Why can't you just be *normal?*"

She stared at him, eyes flashing. "I don't know, Marlboro Man." She flung the daisy cigarette case at him. "Why don't you tell me more about being *normal?*" The case popped open in mid-air, showering him with a cascade of cigarettes. She jerked open the car door. "Go find yourself another beard."

"Lana, come on—" He reached across the seat and grabbed her arm.

"I'm sorry, I didn't mean—"

"I kept *your* secret!" She was crying now, wrenching away from him, struggling with the door. "Just be a fucking gentleman and keep mine."

"Lana—" He pulled her closer and she swatted him across the face with her nails, gouging three deep streaks across his cheeks. He roared in surprise, pain and shock making him grab her forearm harder than he meant.

A familiar dented woody van and its jerry-rigged radio antennae zoomed to a stop right behind them, skidding so close the bumpers almost touched.

Ron whirled. *No*, he thought, *not today.*

He stormed out of his car, blood up.

"You fucker," he growled.

"It's Rockwell's tip," said Darkroom Louie. "Don't shoot the—" Ron roared out of the car and swung a wild punch that got Louie in the ear. To his surprise Louie punched back, a knock in the kidneys that made him double over the hood. "Come on, Ron." said Louie. "We go too far back for this."

"I swore you'd get yours the next time I saw you," said Ron, lunging at him, pushing him against the car. Louie struggled, headbutted, tried to knee him off of him as the two men rolled around the chassis. He flipped Ron over onto the trunk but Ron landed one square uppercut from below, knocking Louie onto the asphalt. The camera strap around his neck broke and something shattered deep inside the black box as it bounced on the ground.

Ron reached for the ruined camera when the kick of an engine made both men look up. She'd slid to the driver's seat, keys still in the ignition.

"Lana. LANA!" Ron shouted. He grabbed at the rear of the car, the smooth metal squeaking on his sweaty palms as Lana sped away on three good wheels and one sparking, naked rim. She careened through a honking, crowded red light and out of sight.

"Get in," said Louie, grabbing the door handle. "We'll run her down."

He opened the door but Ron grabbed him again, slamming the door shut with Louie's body. "You touch her and I'll break more than your camera," he growled.

"Buddy, I was on assignment to get happy pics of the expectant couple leaving the doctor's office." He shrugged Ron's hands off of him. "But now, I'm going to track down your, uh, *excitable* bride. Or someone else is going to." He scooped the camera off the ground, gave it a diagnostic shake, then threw it, disgusted, on the front seat of his car. "She got you good, you know that?" Louie pointed to Ron's face. Ron dabbed at the sore spots with his fingertips. Blood.

"Happy pictures of the expectant couple leaving the doctor's office," Louie sighed, opening the back door and unsnapping a small hard black case. "Rockwell is going to take the cost of my good camera *and* my day fee out of *your* paycheck." He strung the backup Leica around his neck and jumped into the driver's seat. "Get in. You can tell me what the fight was about on the way."

Ron slid in the passenger side. "I'm not telling you anything."

"Dickie, Dickie, Dickie," Louie smiled at him and shut the door. "You say that like I don't already know."

19

They sped down Palm Drive on her trail, Ron scanning the horizon, Louie fiddling with the modified knobs and dials soldered into his car radio. The red line of the dial cranked higher than the music stations and the hiss and crackle of LAPD dispatchers bobbed to the surface of the AM netherworld. Squad cards squawked about purse snatchers and streetwalkers. No chatter about a blonde in a busted Cadillac.

"You know where she might be going?" asked Louie.

Ron thought it through. *Not home*, he thought. *She's still too mad at me. Not to the studio, or her agent—she doesn't trust either of them.* He rubbed the sore spot between his eyebrows. *Who does she trust? Where will she feel safe?*

It dawned on him. "Make a left on Wilshire," he said. "We're going east."

"Just like old times, eh?" said Louie.

It took a moment for Ron to realize what he meant. Back rooms in West Hollywood pool halls, clandestine camera club photo sessions for discerning "hobbyists". He remembered being fresh off the bus and the *psst, want to make a buck?* come-on on Hollywood Boulevard and how hungry he was, how the old men put a drink in his hand and said *relax, pal, it's just photos*. He made a buck, all right, the times he could stomach the thought of their putrid hole of a mouth around him. Only the guy who ran the darkroom in the back ever waved the worst ones off. *Hey, Pops*, he'd call out, *you know what comes after f-stop? F-you. Knock it off, the kid's not interested.*

"Further than West Hollywood," Ron said. "East LA. She wants a drink and she'll be happier in a Spanish-speaking bar."

"Ah, a match made in heaven." The drinks flowed in the back room. The darkroom guy had to scrape him off the floor one night and dragged him to his house. Dickie came to on his couch. In those days, waking up in a stranger's living room wasn't as disorienting as finding himself dressed and unmolested when he did. The guy had a darkroom there, too. *Come on down, pal. Just don't hit the basement lights.* Dickie felt his way down the wall to a black-painted door erected halfway down the flight of stairs. *Watch your step. Five more to go.* He felt for the edge of each stair tread before stepping down in the velvet-thick dark and didn't fully exhale until his footfall landed on concrete and another doorknob nudged into his hip. He turned it and entered the narrow cinderblock room behind the second door, one of those skinny California basements half the footprint of the floor above it. One red bulb lit a lurid monastery space full of low narrow tables lain with rippling shallow trays of vinegary liquid. An enormous vertical cannon barrel of a photo enlarger was tucked away behind a black velvet curtain in the corner. Curling wet papers hung close to the ceiling on crisscrossed laundry lines, like a cavern full of ivory bats. Their folds hid pornographic secrets in high contrast black and white: girl-on-guy and guy-on-guy and girl-on-herself-with-a-whip. There was the soft sound of ever-dripping water.

Hey, it's the morning glory. Rise and shine. Louie nudged a developing print back and forth in the tray before him, grays blooming on the slick paper like a time-lapse bruise. *Here's looking at you, kid.* He nipped the corner of the print with his tongs and held it high, drizzling. Sure enough, there was Dickie in the print, shirtless, nearly pantsless, a strange man laboring over his groin, a photo memento from a moment of his life he didn't remember. The tart air in the windowless room caught the inside of his nose wrong. *How can you breathe down here?* he coughed to Louie.

Why, 'cause it'll make me sterile? Too late for that. He tapped his neck. *Mumps.* He shook the last drops off of the print of Dickie and fellator and clothespinned it high above.

Dickie looked around Louie's lair. There were another set of photos thumbtacked reverently to a section of corkboard across the room. Los Angeles portraits: diner waitresses with solid dignity, pachucos in zoot suits, gin

149

blossom drunks with Faulkner tucked under their arm. *Wow,* Dickie said, *these are really good.*

I admire people who are exactly who they are, said Louie. *You don't get much of that in Los Angeles these days.* He wiped his fingers off on his khakis and wriggled around the tightly packed tables to where Dickie was standing. *See, look at her.* He pointed to a photo of two women standing behind a Helms Bakery truck parked for delivery on some suburban street. The wagon's back was thrown open, packed with candy-colored sacks of soft fresh bread, and the blonde with her hair in a braided crown was throwing open her jacket in the same way, letting the delivery guy in white hat and shit-eating grin get a good double eyeful of her soft white goods. The other stringy-haired woman in a misbuttoned cardigan stared askance into the camera, her thin ankles worrying against each other. She clutched the strap of a round hatbox dangling in front of her knees with white knuckles. *I've known both of them for a long time,* said Louie, *before both were whores, even.* He pointed to the blonde with the open blouse. *Mildred is 'Ruby'. She's living her own delusion, like everyone else in this town. But Dorothy*—he flicked the picture of the lean gal with his fingernail—*is still Dorothy. That hatbox's filled with dope works and pigeon feathers. She is who she is.* His face wore a smile of guarded admiration. *Some people lose the choice when they get here. They get swallowed up by this place.* He looked upon Dorothy the inviolate junkie with reverence. *That's why I respect the people who stay true.*

Dickie regarded Mildred's round and alien breasts. He turned to Louie. *You're not queer, are you?* Dickie asked.

Nope, said Louie. laying another sheet of paper into the basin of developer. Dickie pointed to the portrait wall. *Why don't you do photos like this all the time—you know, instead of the stuff we do—if you're not queer?* Dickie asked, and with a deep sigh Louie replied *I am an impartial chronicler of human behavior. It's just that some human behaviors pay more than others.*

Louie interrupted Ron's reminiscence. "And who's going to get her out of that bar? She's not going to be happy to see either of us."

Ron snorted. "Doesn't that work out better for you?"

"True. We're not quite even yet. You've got about a thousand dollars to go." He flicked a piece of lint off his shoulder. "I'd just bought that enlarger, too." When the heat came down on the camera club racket Dickie choked when a cop gave him the beatdown, threatened to send his "modeling portfolio" to the newsroom of the *Armonk Gazette.* Dickie squealed the address on Norton Avenue, and when the cops roared up to Louie's house they cleared out everything in the darkroom for evidence.

"Louie, that's half a week's salary for me now." Ron reached in his suit pocket. "I'll write you a check today."

Louie smiled but his eyes went into Ron like needles.

The radio crackled alive. "Abandoned vehicle at Pico and Valencia, fifty-eight Cadillac Coupe DeVille, tan, rear flat—"

"She didn't make it past the Pasadena Freeway," said Louie. "Hang on."

They took a hard right and skidded south.

"So here's how I see it," said Louie. "She's gonna be mad. We can do a 'kick-and-screamer'—you know, you dragging her out of the bar. If you get her under the armpits from behind, you won't hurt the baby. I can see both your faces that way, too. Easy, Ron," Louie warned as the car rounded the turn. "You can punch me now, but you don't know what negatives I still have back home."

"We don't know she's in a bar."

"Well, keep an eye out. We might find one to put her in. Not one with neon signs, though, they don't photograph well in daylight. Come on, let me through," Louie cajoled to the cars backed up in the left turn lane. He popped the spool out of the bottom of the Leica and started rooting around in a bag at Ron's feet. "You gonna let me in, buddy? I can't believe this."

"So much for being the impartial chronicler of human behavior."

Louie turned to Ron and fixed him with a hard glare. "I only play fair with those who play fair with themselves, pal. I decided that a long time ago."

"You don't know Lana—" Ron started, but was interrupted by a patrolman bursting through the static. "Pico-Union, we have a visual on the abandoned vehicle, also APB for white female, expecting, possible three-nine-zero, calling an ambulance—"

"That's it." Ron grabbed the bag, ripping it away from Louie's fist. He yanked open the door and stalked out into traffic. Louie quickly exited the car and followed him.

"Come on, Ron," said Louie, waving him back. "This is silly. I've got more film in the trunk," he said with a nonchalance that suggested he didn't. "Let's just get in the car and—oh, come on!" he yelled as Ron wound up like a fastball pitcher and hurled the bag as far as he could. Canisters of 35mm film spun out of the sack and rained down on the road.

"Go get it, Weegee," Ron snarled. Louie jolted away from the car, desperately trying to round up the bouncing cylinders. Ron didn't hesitate. He sprinted to the driver's seat, grabbed at the keys still in the ignition, tore off into a screeching U-turn before Louie could stop him.

"That's the wrong way, you jackass!"

No it's not, thought Ron. His hands were shaking as he gripped the wheel. He had a plan. It would mean outrunning Louie and his bloodhound instincts, outrunning the police, outrunning every tipster and snoop and tourist with a camera. He was going to lure Lana out, and he knew exactly who could do it.

20

The lights hung over the set on Stage 18 like steel vultures. Ron flinched as he walked under them. He hated soundstages. He'd seen a best boy get beaned by a klieg once, the blood pooling between the black snaking wires criss-crossing the floor, like panes of stained glass. Usually he'd be a few cocktails in to cope with their looming presence. Today only determination—and a five spot for the lot guard—pushed him under their leaden glare.

Clouds of dry ice spilled from the catwalks, enveloping Ron in milky cascades of smoke. He brushed through the curtain of chilly vapor and scanned the soundstage. They'd done up the set as a mad scientist's laboratory, with plaster cobblestone walls and beakers bubbling with tinted water and rows of meaningless machines. A Jacob's ladder sent a streak of purple electricity up its wiry V, like a zapping metronome, in time with Ron's pounding heart.

He found him. He was sitting in a canvas chair in full monster makeup, bolts on his neck, shirt artfully torn by wardrobe, mouthing words from a well-thumbed script. The dull pea-green greasepaint smeared across his face just made his blue eyes sharper.

He stood, transfixed, until the whisper echoing through the room broke his hypnosis. *Ron Dash? What's he doing here? Is he doing B-pictures now?* The boy looked up.

"I need your help," said Ron.

Fear? Awe? Hate? It was impossible to tell what the boy's wide-eyed expression meant. Something was wrestling inside him, something that remembered broken noses and sweet rumpled sheets and abandonments over sticky breakfasts. Something that hadn't wised up all the way, yet. Ron leaned in closer. He wanted to put his hand on his— hell, put his hands on *him*, his *mouth* on him, anywhere, now, now, *now*. The script girl, a frowning matron with a plasticized coiffure and cats-eye spectacles, was watching. She had her pencil ready to spot any jump in continuity, in life or art, and as she appraised the two men with a suspicious glare Ron knew what to say.

"Come on," he said. "You've been waiting for me."

They ran to the car. Darkroom Louie had a bag of lens cleaner rags in the back seat. Flaco wiped the greasepaint off his face and said "I can't go out like this."

Ron hesitated, then pulled off his sports jacket, peeled off his dress shirt, stripped off his undershirt. He handed the shirt to Flaco. The boy slid his lean torso into the cotton still warm from Ron's body.

The assistant director appeared at the doorway, irate. "Where the hell is that Pace Hammond kid?" The lot guard pointed towards the car but it was too late, the Coupe DeVille had already screeched out of the lot.

They sped off, back towards East Los Angeles, Flaco in the front seat, Ron trying as hard as he could to keep his eyes on the road.

"I tried to find you," he blurted.

"You succeeded." His words were crisp and precise, unblurred by wetback syntax.

"No," said Ron, and then bit his tongue. Then he thought better of it and spoke. "I called the hotel. But you had already gone."

"They fired me when I came back from the diner with you." Flaco picked at the latex bolts on the soft skin of his neck, wincing as he pulled one loose from the spirit gum glue. "I lost my job and my bed. Well," he said, with a bitter little laugh, "it wasn't my bed to begin with."

Ron remembered how curt the day manager had been to him on the phone, hiding his jilted pride beneath moral outrage. *Hypocrite,* he fumed.

"I tried to find you, too," said Flaco. He tossed the bolt out the window, started picking at the other one. "I read every article I could find about you. I saw Rockwell's name in one magazine. I sent you a letter, through him. One thing led to another . . ." He trailed off. "You didn't even say you knew me, that afternoon in Rockwell's office."

"I couldn't."

"To *Rockwell?*" Flaco glared at him, sapphire eyes judge and jury.

Ron shook his head, the shackles of thirty-six years of shame strangling his words. "You don't understand." The sudden recollection of everything Rockwell's starmaking process entailed inflamed him with swift jealousy. "You can't trust Rockwell," said Ron. "He's using you. He's using all of us."

"He gave me a place to stay."

"His place, I'm sure."

"He gave me diction lessons, taught me proper English. He took me to the *dentist*. My own father never did that."

"He fixed your nose, too."

"I didn't want him to." He yanked the second bolt off of his neck and flicked it out of the window. "I wanted to have something to remember you by."

Ron said nothing. They crossed into Pico Union, noble and decrepit Victorian hotels brooding like mother hens over the low-slung liquor stores and bodegas at its feet. Mexican day laborers clustered in dusty clothes. The sun was setting, the fires under the grills of the *carne asada* vendors glowing tangerine in the fading twilight. The police radio crackled and crossed waves with a low watt *mariachi* station. Ron twisted the dial but couldn't restore the clear-voiced dispatcher.

"You ever see a chicken gets its throat cut?" said Flaco.

"Yes," said Ron.

"When a chicken bleeds? That's nothing. When I was little there was this guy," said Flaco. "He worked the strawberry field with me and my family one summer. He stayed in his shack when all the men were out drinking at night, minding his own business. He read movie magazines, in English. The other men didn't like that." He looked away from Ron, out the window. "I went outside one morning and the ground was wet like mud. They'd bled him out, like a pig. It got on my shoes. I'd smear berries on the stains so I could pretend it was just juice. When I outgrew the shoes my sister got them. Then my brother. Then my other brother." He worried the hem of Ron's undershirt, twisting it in his hands. "I couldn't escape that man's blood for seven years."

Ron couldn't speak.

"I didn't even know what *maricon* meant, I was so little," Flaco continued. "He was nice. He'd given me magazines. I cut out the pictures for the wall of our shack. My *papi* made me take them all down. He made me burn all of them. I kept one picture."

Ron swallowed hard, remembering Tyrone Power. "I remember those photo magazines," he said, throat dry. "They mattered."

"I kept a picture of you," said Flaco.

A small crowd milled at the corner of Pico and Valencia. A police officer stood by an abandoned cream Coupe DeVille, one blown tire making the car slump against the gutter. Ron saw it and darted his eyes around the four corners of the intersection. Where was she?

"Are you taking me somewhere to fuck me?" said Flaco. There was no hope in his voice, just a matter-of-fact bitterness.

"No," said Ron.

"That's a shame," said Flaco. "My lunch break's almost over." For a frightening second Ron only saw Pace

Hammond, the creation tumbled into icy smoothness by the Hollywood machine. "You can take me back now."

"No," said Ron. "I need you. Please. Lana's gone missing."

"Your wife? *Psssssh.*" The hiss of dismissal almost disguised the hurt in his voice. "Why should I?"

"She's pregnant. She's not in a good state. Come on." Something flashed across Pace's face and Ron saw Flaco again, the vulnerable kid at the coffeeshop who'd gotten his heart broken by the last movie star to forsake him. Then it faded and something cruel twisted his face.

"You have to do something for me," said Flaco.

Without warning he slid his hand across Ron's chest and inside his jacket. Ron almost jumped the curb as Flaco's slim fingers crept into his inside pocket and pulled out a pack of cigarettes. He pulled a cigarette out with his lips and let it dangle as he punched the car's cigarette lighter.

"Burn me," he said.

The blood rushed to Ron's groin. He swallowed hard.

The dispatcher's voice burst through the mariachi music. "White female under the Harbor Freeway at Pico Boulevard. Sending ambulance."

"And you'll go get her?" said Ron. "And you'll bring her back here?"

"I'll be yours," said Flaco. "I'll do whatever you tell me to."

Tell her I'm running away with you. Tell her I want you more than I've wanted anyone else in my life. Tell her I'm sorry I dragged her into this lie. Tell her I want her to be happy. Tell her I've branded you and you're finally, finally mine.

"Tell her I'm sorry," said Ron, tongue thick. "Tell her she can have the baby any way she wants. Tell her she can work this out." He grabbed Flaco's forearm. "Tell her in Spanish."

The lighter popped up with a *ping*.

Flaco pulled the chrome lighter out of the socket, not taking his eyes off of Ron. The overpass loomed ahead, a concrete canopy rearing up in the windshield. The *tsss* of red hot tightly coiled metal on tobacco. Ron could see her now, her tiny, tottering silhouette hugging the concrete wall. There was something in her hand. There was an ambulance siren in the distance, getting closer. Flaco pointed the cherry end at Ron.

In one swift move Ron swerved the car hard against the curb and grabbed at Flaco, tore at his shirt, put his mouth hard over his. "You are mine," he whispered into his mouth. He ground the hot tip into the unmarked flesh of his chest, and god, the smell, the sound of the sizzle and Flaco's satisfied yelp, he wanted to fuck him right there, in the car, now, now, now—

He reached across the seat and with superhuman effort yanked the handle and shoved Flaco into the street, away from him. "Get her," he commanded.

The bright look in Flaco's eyes was unmistakable. It was the joy of a dog sent out after a stick, at his master's pleasure. He scrambled to his feet and, dusting himself off, trotted over to Lana.

Ron sat in the front seat and gripped the steering wheel hard. He willed himself not to look at Flaco. He looked only at Lana, at how she turned at the sound of Spanish, how she regarded Flaco with alarm and then clarity, how whatever he was saying was softening her features as she glanced over to the car, angry resolve melting into vacillation. Flaco was gallantly offering his elbow. She took it, and walked back to the car with him. Ron rolled down the window.

"Are you all right?" said Ron. "Come on, give me that." He reached for the paper bag in her hand and saw with some relief that the pint of schnapps was still nearly full.

"We've made a mess of this," said Lana. Her cheeks were streaked with teary mascara.

"I know."

"*You've* made a mess of this," she said, face clouding again. "I think it's best if you're not around any more."

The ambulance roaring closer was visible under the bridge now, a squat brown tank of a car with a white-gowned emergency worker in each front seat. A man in civilian clothes hung on the running board, big flash camera at the ready. *Darkroom Louie.*

He saw it now, the shutterbug hell-bent on revenge for stealing his scandalmobile, the right pictures spinning a damning story in the tabloids: Lana the lush momma, Ron and new face in suspicious clinch, the whole house of lies burying them in crashing timber. He was the rotten beam at the center of it all, the sick fool who brought nothing but pain to the people around him.

Suddenly he saw a way out.

"This is what you're going to tell Louie, and the ambulance drivers, and everyone," he said to Lana, "and I promise either of you will never see me again." He whispered quickly in her ear, then turned to Flaco. "Forgive me," he whispered into his perfect seashell of an ear, and ran off into the night.

21

DO TELL SPECIAL EDITION!
LANA ARLEAUX IN LIFE-OR-DEATH MAMA
DRAMA: "I JUST WANT MY BABY TO LIVE!"
DO TELL CAMERAMAN TO THE RESCUE!

Faithful readers of DO TELL know our crack force of roving journalists, photographers, and invisible army of tipsters never sleep when it comes to digging up delicious dirt in that sin-sational Shangri-La of Hollywood, U.S.A! But this time one of our own—crack lensman Louis "Darkroom Louie" Kowalczyk—was on hand to save expectant mother Lana Arleaux from a near-fatal complication!

The incredible life-or-death yarn begins on an ordinary Friday, as our hard-working snapsman is enjoying his day off by taking photos of local songbirds for his birdwatching album. But when he recognizes a swank Coupe DeVille grounded at a curb in dicey Pico Union, however, suddenly Louie realizes something's amiss with our little miss!

"I'd recognize that Coupe, and its license plate, anywhere," said Louie. "It could only belong to Ron Dash. But it had blown a tire, and there wasn't anyone at the wheel." (LEFT: Police scratch their heads over missing starlet's ride.) Suspicious, Louie tooled down Pico Boulevard until his suspicions were confirmed: A very pregnant Lana Arleaux, stumbling under the Harbor Freeway and weaving back and forth like a tapestry maker in Times Square traffic!

"I'll confess I suspected the worst," said Louie, and we know that you, dear reader, are thinking the same: oft-married, oft-harried Lana's had a past so checkered you can scream "King me"! Could this be a sign the formerly soggy starlet's back on the booze?

"I'll confess, that was my first thought," said Louie. "But I know what a swell job this gal has been doing cleaning up her act since marrying Ron Dash. And when I pulled up beside her, her complexion was as gray as a Seattle day. So I acted on my instincts and called an ambulance."

It's good you did, Louie, because our mother-to-be was suffering from a diabetic spell brought on by pregnancy. A quick trip to the emergency room—and a nice tall glass of California-grown orange juice—set our lady right!

"I'm so grateful to Louie and everyone at Central Receiving," said Lana from her hospital bed. "You've got a real prince on staff, DO TELL. If the baby's a boy we'll name him 'Ron Jr.'—but if not, how do you like the name 'Louise'?"

But that's not the end of this strange stork tale, dear readers! Who do you think was holding Lana's hand in the back of the ambulance? Savvy starwatchers would guess Lana's hubby Ron Dash, but you amateur astronomers would be wrong. It was none other than new teen sensation Pace Hammond, who just happened to be in the predominantly Hispanic barrio of Pico-Union!

"I never had Latin-style food until I came to Los Angeles," said the all-American heartthrob. "Now it's a tradition for me to bring *churros*—Mexican doughnuts— for all my friends at the studio, especially my co-star Tammy Clover. She loves sweets!" (Is that *all* she's sweet on, Pace?)

"But when I heard the ambulance sirens I rushed outside. And when I saw it was Lana, I knew I had to help." This teen Galahad rode all the way to the hospital with Lana—and stayed by her side when doctors gave her a clean bill of health! (She even got her own taste of a piping-hot cinnamon *churro*—Tammy, you'll just have to wait your turn!)

Well, all's well that ends well for momma and baby— but where was Ron Dash during this scare? Turns out he was hard at work on last minute re-shoots for the eagerly anticipated big screen debut of limey spy Clive McQueen in GOD SAVE MCQUEEN. Well, where ever he is tonight, I'm sure he's sleeping well knowing mother and baby are safe as can be!

22

Pace Hammond haunted Ron's dreams that night. He stole in like an incubus with a fistful of skeleton keys, worming his way through one thrashing, guilty nightmare after another. Pace Hammond at the beach, sinew and cinnamon poured into candy stripe swim trunks, a crowd of apple-cheeked teenagers frugging and twisting against frothing surf behind him. "We're having a weenie roast, *señor.*" Driftwood stick skewering a plump red frankfurter. Fat Dickie Vleck, a pimply lump of white suet nodding like an imbecile at how cool and fresh and sweatless Flaco looked against the tide. Flaco's face descended over his for a kiss like the sun blotting out the moon and Ron awoke in a breathless thrash of bedclothes. He unwound his legs from the yanked-out sheets and tried to bury his face on the cool side of the pillow before the dreams bubbled up in the pressure cooker again.

They'd believed him, every word of it, at Do Tell headquarters. He'd called anonymously, spun the whole yarn that made Lana and Louie and Flaco look good. He even put in a detail about a half-drunk bottle of rye in the front seat of Louie's car and reefers in the ashtray in case Louie needed a little extra persuasion to agree to run Ron's version of events—with a few judicious edits, of course. Lana hated him and Louie probably hated him and Flaco had reason to hate him. He'd kept Rockwell's orchestration of their lives intact and ruined everything for himself. It was a lie that would hold as long as he wasn't around to undo it for himself again. Then he caught a cab to Venice Beach and used the key the boy hustler had left behind to get back into the forsaken motel room. He figured Rockwell wouldn't mind. He bought his own bottle of schnapps and downed it. The nightmares still split his brain.

He dreamed again, fitfully. Red carpet premiere, spotlights and flashbulbs going *snap!* and *fzzzzz*, Lana on his arm, snowy and blonde in ice diamonds and ermine, his own tuxedo crisp, his ankle weighted down with a slave manacle dragging a sled dog team of babies. They cooed and burped and crawled their soft little knees over the smashed snowfall of exploded flash bulbs littering the red carpet, like a dusting of hoary frost on a river of blood. "Don't let them play there!" he gasped, aghast at the babies' skinned dimpled knees. "Lana, don't you see—" And then he looked up and saw Lana was not looking at him. Her face was craned up with the rest of the crowd, their jaws agape, cringing in horror as if Godzilla was crowning the skyline. The marquee, craning out like the prow of the

Titanic, spelling out the source of their revulsion in letters tall enough to blot out the sun: RON DASH IN . . . PACE HAMMOND.

And then with the ding of elevator doors Flaco was there, blue eyes in that brown face like sapphires in molten bronze. "Try this on," said Monsieur DuPuis as he girded a tall choker studded with eye-scratching diamonds around Flaco's tender neck. Flaco's hands flew up in self-protective surprise but he didn't cry out as DuPuis clasped the heavy buckles on the nape. A fat silver ring hung from the front of the collar, the kind of loop bulls wear in their nose. Ron reached forward and hooked his finger experimentally against the metal, tugging it, feeling how the chain mail of gems gave slightly as it corseted the boy's neck, watching the boy swallow hard with each tug.

"I can change the mount," said DuPuis. "Some boys feel confined by a choker."

"That won't be necessary," mused Ron with great pleasure. The boy was on his knees now, framed like a bug in a specimen jar in the stark jeweler's spotlight overhead, breathing hard, hands behind his back. He was naked now, chest dotted with keloid scars like a perverse planetarium show, diamonds glittering hard like flecks of glass in the eye, cock stiffening slightly between his coppery thighs. Ron circled him, relishing his discomfort.

"I'd like a very special piece of jewelry for this one," he said, and suddenly DuPuis placed the red velvet box in his hands. He opened it. A slender stickpin, a fierce orange gem smaller than a dime, surrounded by a ragged ring of salt and pepper gems. "This is citrine," said DuPuis, fingers fluttering at his handiwork, "encircled by thirty steel-grey diamonds. A curious palette for a stickpin, Mister Dash—and not much call for grey diamonds, I must admit. But you requested them specifically. Why?"

Ron smiled. "Because it looks like the tip of a cigarette," he murmured to himself.

He lifted the stickpin from the box and there was Jimmy Lariat bound in the back of the barn, Tijuana complexion and eyes *agua azul*. His dark hair hung in his face and his arms were bound back tight and as Ron brought the stickpin close Flaco kicked his cowboy boots and pleaded *ay dios mio . . .* and as he speared the boy's flesh with the prick of the pin there was the salty hiss of sweat and the sizzle of meat on fire . . .

Ron awoke. The motel room was small and ugly and the silence terrified him. He grabbed at the phone as if it were a live grenade tossed in his foxhole, frantic fingers chasing the holes in the dial as they ticked out the one number that could save him.

"Sid Moskov's residence," the gum-chomping answering service girl.

"Ron Dash. Connect me now. *Now*," he growled, and heard the girl curse as the wire clicked over. Three tense rings before Sid picked up with a sigh.

"No comment," he growled, throat full of just-awoke gravel. "Now, who is this?"

"It's Ron Dash, Sid."

"Ron Dash." The sandpaper on Sid's tongue couldn't hide the glow of paternal pleasure in his voice. "Last time

I saw you we were having drinks by the pool and that *ferschlugginer* earthquake hit. How *are* you?"

"I need work."

"Sure, sure. But I'm confused—I thought you had that spy picture all tied up? I read in the trades they're sending you to Jamaica in the spring."

"Listen." Ron's voice hit a fever pitch. "That's then. I need *now*. I don't care if it's television or theater or a goddamn potato chip commercial—as long as it's far away from Hollywood I'll take it."

"Ron, I'm a producer, not an agent." Concern waxed Sid's voice. "Shouldn't you talk to Rockwell about this sort of thing?"

"Rockwell can't know."

The silence on the other end of the line got heavy for a moment.

"Ron," said Sid gently, "are you in some sort of trouble?"

Shit. He'd overplayed his hand, gotten too desperate. Backpedal, full speed. "Of course not." Ron forced out a leisurely chuckle. "Do I sound desperate? It's just with Lana expecting and all, I'm just fretting about being the breadwinner. Guess I've got that new poppa jitters."

"New poppa? *Mazeltov.* Why didn't you say so? Listen, before Mitzie was born I sold three back-to-back courtroom dramas just from sheer terror. I don't even remember the meetings. All I know is once they were all in the can Lou Nussbaum gave me two boxes of cigars—one for Mitzie and one for 'the triplets'." He guffawed. " I've got a few interests. I'll see what I can do."

"But not in Hollywood," Ron stressed. "Anywhere but here."

"Sure, sure. I understand. Guys like Rockwell'll have your hide if he finds out you're on the racetrack when he wants you in the stable. You worry too much, boychik. New additions have a way of working themselves out. It's just been the two of you for so long you can't imagine how three is going to be. Trust me, it's not as crowded as it seems."

Ron thought of Flaco, guiltily. "We'll see."

Hollywood burned like a sinkhole bullseye in Ron's mind, a quake-shaky epicenter that made him shy to leave his room. Joe Crane's? Too hot. Rockwell lunched there on Tuesdays. Same nix on the studio—he might cross paths with Pace, ships in the night on the same vast backlot. No brain-clearing calisthenics in Hancock Park—that's too near where Rockwell fitted him for his first suit, at Falconnier on Wilshire and La Brea. From the shape of that switchblade vent bisecting Pace's lean suitback—Ron gulped a little at the memory—he'd done Pace's Cinderella transformation at the same place. No beach. Pace might be working on a tan. Stay inside, Ron thought. Sit right down and control yourself. And wait for Sid to call.

Finally, the phone rang. "What brand do you smoke? Say Trebuchets."

Ick. Ron looked at the pack of Malta Golds resting on the armchair. "Trebuchets."

"That's what I told them at Geraghty/Klein," Sid beamed. "And that's why you won't get in trouble with the FTC for endorsing the cigarette you already smoke. West

Palm Beach, on a yacht, in a lime grove, and at a supper club. Six days of photo ops, print and billboard. And the money! I'd tell you now but let's put it this way—if Baby goes to Harvard, you're covered."

Gratitude welled in Ron's throat. "Sid, if there's anything I can do—

"A ten-percent finder's fee will set me up right. Plus your undying, dog-like gratitude, but that goes without saying. Ha!" Ron could feel the backslap over the phone. "Have a good time, boychik! Make momma-to-be drink that good Florida orange juice every chance you get!"

23

The tarmac at Fort Lauderdale-Hollywood International was painted citrus yellow. It hurt Ron's eyes. He needed a drink to cool the burn. The stewardess had the do-no-wrong smile of a nursery school teacher. She handed him a scotch and salted peanuts as if it were apple juice and animal crackers. He downed it. She smiled. "Another?" He held out his glass. The tarmac still burned. The seat next to him was empty. He'd even bought a ticket. She didn't come.

"Thank you for flying National, Mr. Dash." She beamed. "It's been a pleasure to serve you."

"Thank you," said Ron. She hovered over his seat for one measured, practiced instant. A gap in time just enough for other men to catch the wink in the offer. Ron felt the weightless moment. He didn't bite. She nodded briskly and stepped away, wide hips kissing each aisle seat in a swaying pendulum gait. He tried to make the sight of her meaty retreating ass do something inside him. He tried real hard.

The cabin door opened. He put on his sunglasses and braced himself.

The humidity hit his face like a smear of ointment. A trio of ad men on the tarmac, hands extended. Dark suits, pastel ties. Sweating just like him.

"Welcome to Ft. Lauderdale, Mr. Dash. Excuse the dust." The tallest of the men waved his hand at the construction nearby. The skeleton of a grand terminal arching out of bare concrete into the bright sun, workmen swarming around like ants denuding a giant carcass in reverse. "The Jet Age needs its cathedrals."

"Don't apologize," said Ron. A colored man hustled to get his bags. "Every airport I landed in today was under construction."

"Our apologies we couldn't fly you directly into West Palm Beach. Uncle Sam still thinks he owns *their* airport. But we'll soon be setting him straight." He gestured to a robin's egg of a car idling on the tarmac, a pretty little Nash made of the same bulbous swerves as the stewardess' hips. "At least this way you'll get to see some of the city." The chauffeur opened the door. "We'll go up Ocean Boulevard. It's a pretty drive."

Dust of the man-made desert around the airport soon gave way to jewels glittering on the horizon, spidery sprays of olive green that became tall swaying coconut palms.

"Most visitors ooh and ahh over the palm trees." One ad man leaned into him, the backslap redolent in his tone. "But they're just backyard trees to you, eh, hombre?"

Ron forced a smile on his face. "I spend more time on sets with fake pines. It's still a thrill to see palms," he lied. Still, privately, he had to admit Florida had the edge on California. California was flat and languid, a desert made into a tinsel oasis. Florida pulsed with chili-hot authenticity. In Hollywood everyone on the street looked like a bit player in someone's massive set. In Florida people looked like they could continue a life offscreen. The buildings were taller and gaudier, Art Deco run amuck in vacation colors. Every laborer on the street looked like Flaco. Loneliness and guilt, the one-two punch that blackened both eyes every single miserable day of his life. *Alcohol*, his heart whispered.

"You look thirsty," the ad man said, proferring a cool tumbler from the minibar. "It's called a mojito. Or a mosquito, depending on how many have bitten you. Think of it as a Cuban gin and tonic."

Gin and tonics made him think of his manager, and how he'd run away without his permission. He downed the drink before guilt could shiv him in the ribs again. This one made a dent in his bad mood, swirled his balance, coated the world behind a haze of liquor. He breathed a tiny sigh of relief, still full of trepidation he'd have to chase this buzz, let it know who's boss. Don't give it any room to breathe, corner it, knock it down, tie it up before it could leave the room. He held out his glass. The ad man refilled it without blinking. Ron suddenly saw how bloated and bloodshot their own faces were, the luxury of self-abuse exercised by men who made their millions without using their face as collateral. He wondered how bad he looked.

"We've checked you in at the St. Antonio. Meet us for dinner?"

"Please."

"We've a full day tomorrow, so soak up the night life tonight." The car pulled up to a hotel curb and a Cuban busboy hustled to retrieve his bags. "You've got a 6 am call. We've rented a charter boat down to the Keys, it'll take us a while to sail there. But until then—" he clapped his hand on Ron's back—"While the cat's away . . ."

Ron's room overlooked the sea, an aquamarine spread of gently coasting waves and little silver parentheses of dolphin, playing in silvery loops. No sunset over the ocean on this coast. He struggled with his tie and somehow got tangled up in it enough to sit down hard on the bed. The ad agency had sent a bottle of rum and a tumble of limes and a spray of fresh mint in a crystal glass. Ron threw the mint on the floor and uncorked the bottle and threw the limes at the wall, one by one, like a kid batting balls against the barn, as he drained one burning mouthful of Bacardi after another. The limes made sorry splats on the saffron colored wall and accumulated in a broken heap on the carpet. The bottle was empty too soon. The four walls of the hotel room started to fold in on themselves like the inside of a piece of paper crumbling.

The telephone sat on the bedstand. He dialed the front desk with thick and disobedient fingers. Call my wife, he imagined his lips saying. *Let her know I've arrived. Let her know I love her and I'm sorry. I'm sorry I scared her in the car. I'm sorry I tried to bully her out of wearing high heels. I'm sorry I slapped her on our honeymoon. I'm sorry about the fight in the car. I'm such a soggy drunk. I'm such a pervert. I'm sorry she ever came in contact with me. I'm so sorry I'm going to walk right into the sea and let the dolphins cavort backflips over my misbegotten body.*

As he lowered the descending rocket of his finger to the phone's dial he felt it coming on, the velvet sweep of the Señor Rum's matador cape enclosing him. The last thing he remembered before blacking out was a sensation like placing down a heavy, heavy suitcase, a relief so palpable it almost made him weep before he blinked out, like a light.

24

Morning came, dead phone still gripped in his hand.

The ad men pretended not to notice how hungover he was, how he'd missed dinner, how there was a pile of bleeding limes in the corner of the room. They poured black coffee down his throat and stuffed him into a white suit and trundled him into the car with a completeness of purpose that scared Ron in his hungover paranoia. They might as well have rolled him in a rug and locked him in the trunk.

He saw the cluck of disdain dying on the tongue of the makeup artist as he patted fleshy concealer under his eyes. The click and whirr of film loading, the snap of lights, the tan-skinned Cubans hoisting gear onto the yacht. The seasick water rolling under the floorboards, the lurch his stomach made left to right. Miserable.

"Look alive, Ron." Ron gave a feeble smile. The ascot around his neck itched. "Someone light his cigarette." A nervous intern stepped forward, his thumb snapping on flint. Ron inhaled and almost gagged. He ran for the edge of the boat and spat grimy, spitty mouthfuls of bile into the ceaselessly rolling water below.

"Jesus," he heard the ad man groan. "Get that poor bastard a hair of the dog."

A mouthwash tumbler of vodka made the lights behind his eyes go on again, made his thoughts bounce softly off the padded walls of the numb space in his head. The wash of the sea against the side of the boat tickled his ears. *I'm on vacation*, he thought, and smiled broadly with sloppy lips.

"That's the movie star smile," he heard the photographer coo, and *snap snap snap*. Each click of the shutter felt like money clattering in the metal winnings bowl of a slot machine.

"They make the bowls out of metal on purpose, you know," Ron slurred. "That way everyone comes running. Everyone hears the big winner."

"Sure, sure." The photographer didn't break stride. "Let's do one with the fishing rod in your hand, huh, Ron?" The assistant handed him the slim fiberglass reel and Ron took it. "You're fishing for marlin," said the photographer. "For swordfish."

"The big game hunter," chuckled Ron. He fumbled with the reel. "With a delicious Trebuchet in hand. Mmm, mmm, that's a mellow smoke."

They got what they wanted out of him. They drove him to a restaurant on the shore and dressed him up in a crisp white dinner jacket and sat him on a veranda, palm fronds swaying. They filled a glass in front of him and Ron took a sip again. This time the medicine didn't take. Something sharp and resentful and sad busted through the surface. His stomach hurt. He realized he hadn't eaten breakfast. He swallowed hard, staring up at the photographer through pained eyebrows. "That's the look," said the photographer and Ron thought, *what, skunk drunk and uncaring?* Snap snap snap. Suddenly wearing the jacket hurt. He fumbled at the black tie at his throat like a circus tiger beating at the wall of its cage and the mood in the room changed. A hushed conference of ad men, a little knot of worried fools waiting for their own ration of iced anesthesia at the end of another miserable day.

"That's good for now, Ron." A hand clapped on his shoulder. Ron flinched. "Let's get some steak and eggs in you. We're going to Hialeah Park this afternoon. You'll love it. The sport of kings." The ad man framed his hands. "Our man, the climbing vines, the flamingos on the infield. You in the stands, a Trebuchet in hand. That's the sporting life. We've even brought in some Tampa thoroughbreds to race in the background, real blue chip beauties."

The thought of racetracks, and Tijuana, and Lana, eyes flashing, the real blue chip beauty, plunged an ice needle of guilt into his heart. The ad man kept prattling on. "The insurance men wouldn't let those horses travel unless the agency sprung for their own private veterinarian *and* a trailer, so he could room next to them, can you believe that? A racehorse's life: travel with your own doctor so you can run like hell a few times and spend the rest of your retirement romancing pretty fillies. Every man's dream. My friend, I think we're in the wrong line of work."

"Order those eggs for me," said Ron. "I'll be back in a moment." He stumbled to the bathroom, splashed his face with cold water, stared in the mirror at his ghoulish face, at the pancake foundation melting onto the lapels of his suit. He stared for a good long time.

"Fuck it," he said.

Bright Miami noon burned like an atom bomb blast. He waved his hand and a taxi appeared, same lascivious pink as the minty indigestion balm from the medicine cabinet. He shut the door and hoped the taxi's obscene color would do the same work on his seething ulcerated stomach.

"Where to, *señor*?" asked the cabbie.

The word stabbed him. *Ay Dios Mio.* "Don't call me *señor*."

"My mistake, mister. Where can I take you?"

"Anywhere."

"You want to see some of Miami Beach?"

"Anywhere."

"*Si*, mister, hold on tight."

The drink in his empty gut roiled around inside him as the cab's manual transmission jerked and started into traffic like a rodeo animal. Ron clutched his hand to his side. Something was different this time, more than the hurt and the burn and the usual daze of hangover. The blackout last night . . . something had gotten loose. Something had slipped out of the wrought iron cage inside him and was now prowling the house of his intellect, knocking over furniture and soiling the floor, gouging great scratches into the foundation. Something that laughed at him. *You can't drug me*, the thing laughed, its smile glistening with great feline teeth. *You try to drown me in booze but I've learned to swim. I'm watching you, Ron. I'm coming for you. And this time I will win.*

"Stop the car," heaved Ron, and yanked open the door.

"Fontainebleau Hotel," the cabbie announced, ignoring Ron retching in the gutter. "Have a pleasant day, *señor*."

The little flurry of whispered voices hit him like sparrows on a windshield, the same flurry that greeted him everywhere. *Ron Dash? Isn't that Ron Dash? He doesn't look so well. He looks taller in the movies. Where's Lana?* The cool blue grotto of the lobby beckoned. He ducked inside.

Fontainebleau. A nonsense word. The carousel of tourists spun around him, sunburned men and women dressed how they thought movie stars dressed on vacation. Hawaiian shirts and cigars, women dangling white rabbit wraps on awkward elbows despite the heat. Their eyes pinched behind dark glasses. The scar marks of lobster red sunburns marring their skin. *Fon-taine-bleau.* Where had he heard that before? It came back to him, a quiet afternoon spent nodding over an architecture magazine and a scotch. Morris Lapidus, brave mad tasteless visionary, the vulgar multimillion-dollar hotel he'd planted on Miami Beach like a space age carbuncle. Ron remembered how the article's author recoiled in horror at the sheer epic vulgarity of Fontainebleau, how it could only appeal to tastes both uncultured and hungry for spectacle, and Ron had chuckled to himself *you mean, to people who go to movies?* Standing here he could see it was true. The entire place had the déjà vu feel of a movie set, and all the tourists milling around and adopting poses waited with the same anxious, expectant attentiveness of extras awaiting direction. He had to turn around to check himself, to make certain just outside this fiction there wasn't the usual army of grips and best boys and makeup artists and the director himself, proud and officious in his canvas back chair, megaphone in hand. *Your motivation in this scene is you are on vacation. You are here with someone you love. You are very, very happy.*

There was an enormous grand staircase in the center of the lobby. Ron's hands gripped the edge of the balustrade and pulled himself up, an act of will overcoming the encroaching edges of a blackout. There was nowhere upstairs he wanted to go. He didn't even know if there was an upstairs. Some magnetic force was pulling him, compelling him, the same force that compels monarch butterflies to migrate north. There was something unique about these stairs—did he remember it from the article? Some nonsensical detail about the hotel that made the reporter spit bile?—and he had to try ascending them himself.

A bellhop appeared almost instantly, a weak-jawed man in the hotel uniform. "Excuse me, sir." Ron swiveled his head drunkenly.

"There's nowhere to go," the bellhop said.

Ron paused. "Excuse me?"

"Where do you need to go?" He gestured to the top. "Those stairs, they don't go anywhere."

"They don't go anywhere," Ron repeated, and then the detail came back to him. *Of course.* Morris Lapidus, famously, foolishly, installed a grand staircase in the center of the lobby and expected the spoiled cattle of American touristry to take the elevator instead. The stairs didn't connect to the second floor. They were an illusion, a false ladder.

Another memory came flooding back. A childhood trip to South Carolina. The hot ride in the car, the relatives smelling like perfumed talc and the two bits placed in his hands when his dirty faced cousins wouldn't play with the sissy and the relatives started whispering about how Yankee life made boys soft like biscuit dough. *Run along to the movies, now,* said his humiliated mother, and he didn't have to be told twice, skipping down the block to Main Street and the glittery embrace of the bijou. Myrna Loy, Clark Gable. He wanted to sit in the balcony. No theater at home had a balcony and the mouth of the worn staircase beckoned invitingly. A bird's eye view of the movies, it promised, a step closer to heaven where the stars live. He lay his sweaty white hand on the banister and a Negro janitor caught him before he ascended the first stair, his heavy palm as big as a palm frond, burning on Ron's chest. *Stop, boy.* The terror in little Dickie's eyes must have compelled the man to soften his stern expression. *You not from around here, huh? Well, you's s'posed to sit in the main theater. Up thar's only for culluds. They tell us it's somethin' special up thar so's we git excited to sit in the balcony. Tain't special. It's just where they put us. They's got a name for it. Nigger Heaven.*

"People think there's something special up there," said the bellhop. "They keep wanting to climb it. They think they'll discover something when they get there." The bellhop shrugged, his eyes wistful. "It's just stairs."

Nothing there. The climb to Hollywood, to stardom. Make money. Get married. Have a child. A stair to nowhere.

"Can I show you to the elevators?" the bellhop said, but Ron was already out the door, running to the beach.

25

Ron stripped off his shoes and ran onto the sand. The sun was setting, obliging the sherbet-colored city with matching hues of raspberry and tangerine and a flash of lime, not at the shore's horizon like in California but ducking behind the skyline like a shy bride. The beach was emptying, the lifeguard stand empty, the crowds long gone inside to swab sunburns and nurse mojitos in preparation for evening. He didn't think to roll up his cuffs as the waves bubbled and kissed at his ankles.

"Lana," he whispered to himself. "I'm sorry."

She would get insurance. He had some. And the house and the car and America's eternal esteem. The tabloids would hound her for a while. *Brave Widow Soldiers On—"At Least I've Our Baby To Comfort Me."* Maybe she'd start drinking again, as if she ever stopped. Maybe she'd suspect the truth. Everyone else would guess it was an accident, and they'd forgive him. They wouldn't blame her for driving him into the sea. No one blames a woman with a baby.

He was up to his waist now. How does one drown? Does it just take will? To ignore the burning in your lungs? Do you need to go out so deep that when your body jerks and hiccups there's no ground to stand? Do you empty your lungs and sink like a stone and peer up at the jade-green expanse above your head, flickering with light and air and second chances far above you . . . and wait?

The water shot cold through his shirt to his nipples. The waves buffeted him and the ocean floor dropped away from beneath his feet like a gallows trap door and by instinct he started to tread water. *The strongest swimmer at the Armonk Y.* His muscles thrashed, twitched, a drowning animal saving itself. He forced himself to stop. The water crept to his chin, to the soft space behind his ears, where only lovers kiss. A wave swelled and crashed down over his head, one final dunk. It was quiet underwater, quiet and green, and the flashing knives of sunlight cut only so far down into the cold.

No. Stop. I want to live, he thought, one moment too late.

26

Hhhhhhhhhhhhuuuuuuuuuuuuhhhhhhh . . .

The crash of the surf cut through the ringing in his ears. Sand, under his palms. Breath, ramming its way back into his burning lungs one tortured gasp at a time.

Breathe in.

Breathe out.

Breathe in.

Am I alive?

There was a hand on his back. A soft voice in his ears.

"It's okay," the voice said, soft and boyish and comforting, its sweetness salted with the trace of a Mexican accent.

Ron looked up.

The blue eyes. The caramel skin, glowing like amber against the periwinkle sky. The crooked nose, set just so.

Flaco.

"What—" croaked Ron. His mind swam with questions his salt-burned throat couldn't voice. *Why are you here? How did you find me? Was it you who saved me?*

Flaco pointed to the shore. "She sent me."

Ron squinted. There, on the beach, a round white egg against the glitter of Miami twilight. White sundress. Full belly. Blonde hair, whipping in the wind.

"Lana?" he gasped.

He could see the crease in her eyebrows as she walked closer, the deep concern underpainting her pretty face. *She is so pretty*, thought Ron, in a way he'd never thought before, and his heart swelled with gratitude.

"Why are you . . ." Ron began and then choked, spat, washed up a mouthful of grit from some forgotten crease in his throat. Flaco put his hand on the back of Ron's neck, gently. Lana knelt, her cool white hands on each side of Ron's face. She lifted his bloodshot eyes to meet hers.

"You called," she said, voice as steady and calm as a mother not wanting to telegraph her fear. "You said you were living a lie and you'd walk into the ocean unless someone was there to stop you."

I called? Ron racked his brain feverishly. The limes yesterday, the blackout, the phone in his hand. Did he dial? Did she pick up? How long had he been thinking about this? A day ago? A week? Since the day he ran away to Hollywood? Since the day he knew he was small and weak and different and condemned to wander the earth without true love?

"But how . . ." Ron looked at Flaco. The thrill of finally staring at his handsome face once more mingled with the guilt of doing it in front of his wife.

"Silly," said Flaco. "She can't save a drowning man in her condition. It's what we do in California, right? Send a Mexican to do the dirty work."

Flaco smiled. "You're lucky I like the dirty work."

Ron pieced it together. "So you came together . . ."

Lana finished the thought. "Because," she said, waving her hand at her pregnant belly, "I can't save you like this. But also . . ." Her face quivered. "I know I can't save you . . . *like this.*" She waved her hand at her belly again. It took Ron a moment to understand why her voice choked as she said it. That belly, those breasts, the life growing inside her. A mother. A woman. Female. She was a beautiful and generous and wonderful human being and she would never, ever be his true love. And she knew why.

And he did too. Tears sprung to his eyes as he imagined the events of the past 24 hours. His sloppy suicide phone call to a pregnant woman who should be getting her sleep. Her getting out of bed, calling favors, tracking down Flaco. Her face-to-face meeting with the man who truly held his heart. Flying down on the red eye, probably on a ticket she bought for the two of them. His wife and his secret crush, working together, tracking down taxis, finding hotels, making a good guess where he was—and never a hint of bitterness or bile from her as she let Flaco save him from the deep in a warm lifesaving embrace.

Gratitude swelled his heart. "Lana, I want to make this up to you."

"You will," she said calmly and evenly. "Good men always do." She tried to hoist herself up off the wet sand, but struggled. Flaco and Ron both offered a steadying hand. She took both. "For now," she said, brushing a strand of wet hair off his forehead, "let's get you cleaned up."

27

Even half-drowned, Ron could spot how thoughts percolated in Lana's brain as she flicked her lighter and barked clipped conclusions to herself. "The ad men are looking for you, correct? So let's go to the South side. Taxi!" She whipped her blonde hair around and a taxi the sunset color of a mango came screeching to a stop.

Flaco steadied Ron into the backseat while Lana leaned in the driver's side window. "¿Puede guardar un secreto?" She tucked a ten into the breast pocket of the cabbie's cubavera. The cabbie waved his cigar at the men in the back seat. "Desde luego," he said. "Hop in."

They peeled out past moneyed palisades, cabana lights washing over them in sherbet strobes. The jouncy ride made Ron carsick, and as he closed his eyes and tried to take deep breaths of the stifling humid air he felt Flaco's hand pat *there, there* on his. That innocent gesture shot through him like lightning. It had been so long since a man touched him. The touch of his flesh elicited equal measures of magnetic exhilaration and shame.

They traveled away from the Art Deco high rises looming over the highway like marble sentries. South River Drive, Little Havana. The road narrowed and squat buildings closed in, like spectators jostling closer. Accordion music, the smell of bread and rum. Cigar factories. Jade-tailed roosters prancing in the street. *Ropa vieja* simmering in pots at takeaway counters and *medianoche* ham-and-cheese sandwiches pressed between hot grills, sizzling their porky perfume into the night.

Lana fanned a stack of bills at the driver. "Shsssh," she pouted as the cab slid to a stop. The driver nodded, *comprende*. She folded the money into his palm and nodded to Flaco and Ron in the backseat. "This is our stop." The strange trio of them—wavering goliath, slim caramel buttress, squat blonde ready to hatch—watched the taxi retreat. When the cab turned the corner, they turned and hustled the other way.

"I don't trust him," said Lana, moving as quickly as she could as she panted for breath. "The less he knows about where we're going, the better." Ron tried to scoop her up— even pregnant he reckoned she'd be a trifling burden in his brawny arms—but she waved him off. "A little further, a little further. There," she said, pointing through the rude mouth of a rough brick alley to a little six room motel on the other side. *Casa De Los Fugitivos*. Even Ron could translate that one.

The desk clerk wiped his face and waved his meaty hands, *no, no, sin vacantes, no room, no room*, but when

Lana waved a stack of bills in his face he whispered something to a unibrowed tough who departed with suavehipped certainty. Soon enough, one moment later a loudly protesting couple—she teetering on one high heel, him frantically tucking in his shirt—paraded past the front window, the unibrowed tough strongarming each of them down the street.

The clerk smiled. "Your room, *señora*."

The room was a grim little affair, turquoise and dank, with strange lacy shadows clustering in the upper corners and one orphan vanity chair in the corner. Lana didn't waste time.

"You'll be sleeping here," she said to Ron.

"What about you?"

"I will sip a long and slow and thoughtful *café con leche* at the bodega around the corner, and then I will take a taxi back to the airport, and return to Hollywood, and make a future for myself."

"What's that supposed to mean?"

She gave him a quizzical smile. Without speaking, she took Flaco's hand and gently clapped it onto Ron's.

"He's all yours," she said, to neither man in particular.

Then she turned for the door.

Ron listened to the sharp clicks of her high heels echo mournfully on the tile floor like pennies dropping into a deep well. She was walking out of his life for good. The failed experiment, the rocket immolating on the launching pad. Everyone knew it was a fool's errand to marry a gay man to a true-blue woman. The zookeepers tried their hybrid and it didn't take, box office receipts be damned.

Better to quit while he was ahead, let her walk out the door so he could tear into the Mexican he'd been throbbing over for months, in private. She retreats to the world of diapers and vacuums and he slides safely back to the dark alleys where dick-hungry men scratch each other's loveless itches. It was sensible. It was rational. It was the only way.

Ron grabbed her arm, hard.

"Don't go," he commanded.

"Stop it, Ron. I know when I'm beat," said Lana. She bit her lower lip. "We had a good run. Let's end this as friends, for the baby's sake."

"Let's end nothing," said Ron. His voice suddenly took on a timbre he hadn't heard in months, full of power and certainty. "I love you, Lana."

"Please, Ron." Her voice was rough and choked, scuffed with impending tears. "Don't . . ."

"Don't what? Don't stand by the woman I love? Don't ask her to be by my side? Don't show her my gratitude for saving my life, in so many ways?"

"I'm a *woman*, Ron."

"You're a person. You're a soul inside a body. And I may not love the body but I sure as hell love the soul."

"You loved the body pretty good," Lana chuckled, fat tears shining down to the corners of her smile.

She was right. Goddammit, she was right. It was easy to forget now, when pregnancy bloated out the sharp right angles of her epicene figure. But he had. He did. Even now, her hair lustrous with hormones, her face cushioned by extra calories, her bustline hillier than it had ever been, he saw the beauty inside. Pregnant, she was as opposite to male as you can get, and the sight of her still made the breath catch in his throat.

"I want to give you a present," he said. He sat her down firmly in the chair and crossed the room over to where Flaco stood obediently. He stood before him, coolly returning the boy's puppy dog gaze. Experimentally, he wrapped his big hands around Flaco's neck as if measuring him for a collar, massaged his thumbs into the soft spot under the jaw where the boy's pulse fluttered, gave his neck a little shake. Flaco didn't resist. He kept staring up at Ron with those big expectant eyes.

"I've given you lots of jewelry," said Ron to Lana. "Lots of pretty pennies worth of precious stones. And I never asked what kind of bauble you like the best." He turned to Lana. "I have an idea now." He stood behind Flaco, placed his hands on his shoulders, pushed him to his knees before Lana like a knight genuflecting before a queen.

She was one sharp tack but it took her a minute. Then the befuddled crease in her forehead melted away and she sank back stunned into her chair.

"You said you always wanted to know how queers did it," said Ron.

"I did," she said, eyes not quite focusing. "But how?"

"I'll show you," said Ron.

Rockwell taught all his actors how to lower their voice to a leading man baritone when the occasion called for it. Ron dredged up the lesson now. "Get on the bed," he rumbled to Flaco, frequency as low as the MGM lion. Flaco jumped like prey and obeyed, stripping out of his t-shirt, wriggling his arms girlishly out of the sleeves instead of pulling it off from the back. That chest again, so young and smooth and rippled with only the faintest sheen of muscle. Ron eyed him coolly as he unbuckled his own belt, relishing the anticipatory slide of the smooth leather out of the belt loops and into his hands. He smacked the gathered leather against one palm, just enough to kiss the flesh. Flaco got the message. Ron pushed him down onto the thin mattress, reaching down to his hips to flip him onto his stomach. His fingers hooked deeply into the waistband of Flaco's shorts.

"Stop," said Flaco.

Ron heard him distantly. The sight and touch of Flaco's trim waist funneling into his tight narrow hips delayed the words to his brain for a hypnotized moment. *Bury my dick in it. Fuck it. Tear into it. Wait—did he say stop?*

Flaco looked up at Lana. She sat, legs crossed as much as she was able, staring a hole into both of them. The expression on her face was impossible to read, but the moment he saw Flaco flash the same near-telepathic look back to her he knew the situation had dissolved out of his hands.

"This is your husband," he said to her.

"That never mattered to either of you before," said Lana.

"Because I didn't think it was real," said Flaco. "Is it?"

Lana didn't say anything. Neither did Ron. Their marital silence was deafening.

Lana waved her hand at the two men. "I didn't come here to watch you hump someone smaller and weaker. Believe me, I've had quite enough of that." She had regained her senses, and her gaze was clear and certain as she rose from the chair and crossed over to the two men. She looked Ron in the eye.

"Surrender, Dorothy," she said.

Something terrifying welled up in Ron. It reared up from underneath movie magazines and unheated garages and men with handlebar moustaches in the Armonk Y. It reared up in the rawest and woundedest part of him. He began to shudder.

"No," he said, punching the bass in his voice so she'd leave him alone.

"Because if you're always the big man," Lana continued, stroking his face and gently guiding Flaco out from underneath him, "you never touch what's real."

"No," said Ron, his baritone slightly aquiver.

"You never get to the core," said Flaco. HIs fingers unbuttoned Ron's collar, skipped like a schoolgirl unbuttoning each in turn, sliding him out of his clothes until Ron was the naked one before him. "You never learn to let go."

He took his face in her hands and stared deeply, compassionately into his eyes. "You have to learn how to love again."

"I can learn how to love."

"To love is to surrender," said Lana. She reached down to the bed and smoothed out the crude sheet with her palms. "And you get to choose your master. You get to choose someone you're certain will hold your heart with care." She looked meaningfully at Flaco. "But ultimately, you have to give that heart to them."

"I'll get hurt," Ron choked.

Lana turned to Flaco. "Will you hurt him?"

"Maybe."

"By accident?"

"That's the risk."

"But never on purpose."

"No." His bright eyes shined brilliant with tears. "I love him."

"I love him too."

There was nothing more to say. The air hung heavy in the silent room. There was a feeling of dawn breaking, of something nervous and new conjuring up inside Ron. It was the *yes* of a coiled seed daring to uncoil and break through the dirt to become one fragile green sprout in the spring. That sprout could become a tree. It could become anything.

Ron took a deep breath, and lay face down on the bed.

Flaco climbed astride him, his thighs straddling the tops of Ron's thighs.

"I will not hurt you," said Flaco, gently.

Ron couldn't say anything. He couldn't breathe. The wrecking crew inside him was breaking plaster left and right, demolishing walls around his heart and setting it free. He had put so many boys here, right where he was now, in the hopes of never being small and victimized again. Flaco's cool girlish hands were creeping under the edge of his belt, gently stroking the skin under his shirt. The boy leaned forward and Ron sucked in his breath as he felt the smooth flat chest press against his back, the hands crest around to palm his nipples, the hot exhalation and gentle kiss the boy bestowed on the nape of his neck. His body stiffened, but, with a great sense of relief, he realized the adrenaline jolt making his body tremble was less fueled by terror and more by anticipation.

He willed himself to relax. He felt the heat of the boy's chest lift off his back, and heard the rustling sail sound of him peeling off his shirt. He lifted his hips and the boy's small hands crept around his waist to unbuckle Ron's belt. He felt a tender, exploratory finger drag across the small of his back and find where the notch of his buttocks began. The boy's finger went deeper.

Ron sucked in a sharp breath of air. In that touch some floodgate opened. A deep sadness welled up inside him, a hurt of self-hate and shame magnified by men hurting him. Men using him. Men treating him as a commodity on the fuck market. He had made himself so big and strong to prevent that ever happening again. He started to sob but the boy didn't stop. He kept stroking, teasing, kneading the soft button of his asshole, pressing his finger against the pucker, not truly penetrating, not yet. The tears poured from Ron's eyes. He turned his face into the pillow to hide and felt another hand caressing his hair. It took him a moment to realize it was not Flaco's hand, but Lana's.

"Ron?" said Lana, softly.

He turned to look at her. Her topaz eyes were twin golden pools of forgiveness. They gave him strength.

"I'm ready," he said.

Lana stepped away. The boy undressed completely and Ron heard every clink of metal buckle and zipper as loudly as if it was a drawbridge opening. The world turned sharp now, every moment in stunning Technicolor relief: the hands diving around to uncinch his belt. The cool, goosepimpling air on his legs as the boy yanked his waistband down to his ankles. The last kiss on his neck, and the way the boy's knees nudged Ron's legs apart. The sound of the boy spitting into his hand. The blunt, warm pressure of the *something* Ron knew could be nothing else, pressing exploratorily against the pucker of his ass. He knew it from the other half of the equation. He knew that door would mercilessly lock unless you found the combination—the correct angle that cleaved boys like a knife in a melon. It took time and experience to find. He wondered if the boy could find it.

He did.

Ron gasped and clutched the sheets. His ass seized up in sudden ricture—the boy wasn't deep inside him, not yet, his frightened body was clamping tight around just the tip, but it was enough to make the boy gasp too and softly swear in astonished Spanish, *ay dios mio* again. Those words reminded Ron of their first encounter. It made him remember the boy felt the same pleasure he felt when he did this to others, and the thought made him ungrip the boy's cock a little. Wait. It wasn't the same pleasure. The pure mechanical pleasure of in-and-out-in-a-tight-space was never the full picture for Ron. He realized now that was part of it, but the other part was a sense of relief, that when safely on top he wouldn't—*couldn't*—be the victimized one underneath.

But Flaco didn't feel that. Ron knew it for sure. He knew it in the way the boy gently gripped his hips and the gentlemanly way he nudged and slid gingerly, probing and massaging instead of reaming. He was safe. Ron could surrender to him. And with that thought, he did. The boy slid in an extra torturously exquisite inch and this time Ron's tears were ones of relief and delight.

"I don't deserve this," he sobbed.

"You do," said Lana, her words soft and gentle and true. "Flaco, *andale*."

Flaco pushed hard and Ron shuddered, his groin shot through with a lightning bolt of pleasure. "Oh my god," he murmured, speaking in tongues as only the deliriously pleasured can. "Oh my god, oh my god, oh my god . . ." Flaco's cock was thumping against a secret pleasure spot inside him, a button of delight Ron didn't know he had. He pushed his hips up against Flaco's, relishing each jolt. Flaco noticed, and took care to draw his cock back against that secret spot, with the maestro delicacy of a violin virtuoso drawing out one long pure note from taut strings. Each push sent a charge to Ron's cock. Each thrust against that secret honeyed spot felt like stroking his cock without stroking it, like invisible tendrils rolling and surging and twining through every ecstasy-glazed nerve.

Suddenly Ron swelled with gratitude. Hollywood was a rough town, and he hadn't realized how much its sharp corners had damaged his soft edges. Here, in this room, were his wife and his lover—two people who had his best interests at heart, who'd forgiven his trespasses, who wanted only his happiness, who cared enough to be gentle where he was gentle and tough where he needed what's tough. That was two more people than he'd ever met in all of his time in the cutthroat sewer of Tinseltown.

The words sprung from his lips. "I love you," he cried out, the declaration addressed to both of them—and maybe, for the first time ever, a little bit to himself. Flaco leaned in, whispered in his ear. "*Tambien te amo,*" he whispered, his voice equally choked with emotion. Ron reached up, grabbed his hand, craned his neck up, his lips meeting Flaco's, their searching lips and tongue finding each other. With a shock Ron realized he'd never once before kissed someone while they were fucking him. The realization made him grab on to Flaco more fiercely, pouring all the love he had into their kiss. He almost didn't hear the phone ring. Its shrill *brrrrrrng* broke the charged air like a cold martini thrown in someone's face. He shot a look at Lana. Lana returned the same scared glance.

Ron picked up.

"I own you, Ron," said the voice on the phone. It was cultured and calm and crackly with menace. "I own you and your wife and especially your concubine."

"Who is this?" choked Ron. His guts clenched up like ice.

"If you think you can run away from the house that built all three of you, I'll ruin you."

Rockwell. "If this is about the cigarette ads—"

"It's about more than that and you know it. I'm tired, Ron. Tired of feeding a stray dog only to find he's poaching from the chicken shack when I'm not around."

"You don't own Flaco." Ron gritted his teeth. "And you don't own Lana or me."

"His name is Pace. Pace Hammond. I made him and built him and yes, he's mine. I'm a funny sort of kid,

Dickie Vleck. When I'm tired of my toys I still won't share them. So I break them before I throw them in the trash. Which is just as well. Because you three were just about broken to begin with."

Ron mouthed *go, go, go* and Flaco jumped off the bed, grabbing his clothes from the floor. Lana darted to the window, straining at the painted shut latch. Flaco ran to her side. Ron didn't need to speak Spanish to understand their frantic chatter. *Miss, you'll never fit through. I will fit. Help me, before they come through the door!*

CRASH! The door broke down in a spray of splintering wood. The paparazzi scrum advanced on them like an aerial raid, a snapping multi-headed monster with sodium flash bulbs burning white dots in Ron's retina.

"We've got you, Ron!" one photographer screamed, triumphant, voice proud with bloodlust. The photographers crowded around them, flashbulbs popping, cameras grinding frames through their unblinking lenses. There were more than a dozen of them, Ron saw now, and where some held cameras others held chains and baseball bats, ready to beat their quarry down if it fought back. "Smile pretty, ladies. Keep your hands where we can't see them." Ron met eyes with Darkroom Louie. It made sense to see the hangman at a time like this.

"Goodbye, Ron," said Rockwell. His voice oozed poison. "Don't fuck with the dream machine."

28

Ron saw the headline in his mind. Black letters tall as a tombstone.

SICK! SICK! SICK!
RON DASH in SICK FAG CLINCH!
WARNING!

We here at DO TELL are made of pretty strong stuff—but this story is so sordid, so vile, so deviant even we hesitate to print it. ONLY OUR COMMITMENT TO TRUTH, DECENCY, and FERRETING OUT CORRUPTION from that wholesome capitol of dreams HOLLYWOOD, U.S.A. stiffens our resolve to print THE UGLY TRUTH! Ladies, beware—we give the facts herein in FRANK and UNVARNISHED truth! You have been warned!

Ron Dash, he-man of dreams, has a big sick secret— and its name is Pace Hammond! Turns out the matinee

McQueen is a REAL queen—and teen heartthrob Pace Hammond is his little "love object"—if you can call what they do together *love*!

"Lover's squabble!"

DO TELL got the down-low on the big sickos when an anonymous source clued our crack team of reporters in to a catty lover's spat squalling up a dive in Cubatown, Miami. Our sources thought there were two cats in heat yowling at each other, the way they were carrying on indecently. Other guests poked their noses into the hall, wondering what in heaven's name made so much noise. Well, heaven had nothing to do with it, as DO TELL found when we pushed down the door!

"Grecian perversions!"

Inside the hotel room we uncovered a den of unprecedented deviance! Ron Dash, as naked as the day he was made, hiding his face in the mattress—engaged in an act so sordid we can't print it here! Suffice it to say the sissies of Socrates day would give a limp-wristed thumbs-up to the godless way Ron Dash got teen star Pace Hammond to *insert* himself into the situation! And who was that perverse distributor of nauseating ministrations? None other than peachy-cheeked Pace Hammond, heartthrob to millions of teenage girls! What's worse, big sissy Dash couldn't cover his face with his hands—*because his wrists were bound!!!*

"A constellation of burns"

When our team of photographers crashed into the room, the two deviants quickly tried to cover up evidence of their sick scene but we were too quick. Most shockingly, we saw a cigarette burning in a nearby ashtray—nothing sinister about that, but our quick-eyed photographers noted a strange constellation of burns across Pace Hammond's back. Could it be that Dash or Hammond get their jollies from *burning each other with cigarettes?!?!* Even more horrific, is this unholy pageant for the benefit of mother-to-be Lana Arleaux?!? What has happened to the flower of American womanhood if instead of crocheting sweet notions for her baby to be, that depraved pinko banshee Lana Arleaux seeks the unholiest and unspeakable of self-gratifications?!?! Feminine self-abuse, back door business, rope handcuffs, and now cigarette burns? Is there no level of depravity to which this satanic threesome will not stoop?

"I weep for them"

Dash and Hammond's agent, the legendary Edgar Rockwell, had no comment. "I'd heard rumors of Ron's extracurricular proclivities for years," said Rockwell with a sad shake of his head, "but I dismissed them as the sick slander of other deviants jealous of his awesome gifts. But to find out that they're true . . . and it's doubly sad when boys in this town don't have the moral compass to say no to the occasion of sin. May God have mercy on their souls." It goes without saying that Rockwell's dropped both ex-stars from his payroll, and Arleaux's agent is not returning calls.

"Not in this town"

But Dash and Hammond aren't done paying the piper. When word of their deviant little party reached LAPD, they let it be known they're filing sex perversion charges for both men, and investigating possible deportation proceedings for Mexican-born Hammond. Guess the newest prisoners down in the sissy wing at Alcatraz will be these two Hollywood pervs! "We don't tolerate perversion in this town," said a grim-faced LAPD chief—and we don't tolerate it here at DO TELL! The mere mention of this kind of sick

DASH continued page 4

LANA ARLEAUX—IN THE PINKO?!?

Ron Dash's secrets run deep—sources now intimate that left-leaning Lana Arleaux is a big fat pinko—a card-carrying Commie with years of documented subversive activity. Looks like Mr. and Mrs. Dash had a good laugh at America's expense covering up their secrets! DO TELL uncovered photos of a "worker's party" meeting in San Francisco in 1942 where Mrs. Dash—then "Victoria Anne-Marie Schultz," is photographed hoisting a sign with the Communist flag at a labor rally. That photo led to the revelation that J. Edgar's got a thick dossier on

Little Miss Hammer And "Sickie," and it doesn't look good: distributing pamphlets decrying our American way of life, making speeches in private meetings lionizing commie leaders, and worst of all, pledging a meaty chunk of her Hollywood salary—*your* ticket money—to Castro's revolution in Cuba! Twisted invert Ron Dash has a whole heaping helping of dirty laundry in the public eye to 'splain away, but just ask the Justice Department: swishy tricks might get you locked up in the booby hatch, but that's nothing compared to out-and-out treason. Should Lady Liberty pick the gas chamber? Or the electric chair? Choices, choices! What's a girl to do? Let's hope Lana's got a few friends left—she's going to need them!

29

"You bastards . . ." Lana stood up. Some photog, some beefy, stubbly thug Ron had never seen before gave Lana a *come, come now* sneer. He put his big salty mitt all over her face and sat her down hard. Ron's blood surged to his fists. Two toughs saw the tsunami coming and linked elbows with him, the three of them do-si-do partners at the world's roughest square dance.

The thug strode over to Ron. One, two. Gut punches sent a knot of vomit into Ron's throat. He collapsed against his captor's arms and tried not to be sick all over his feet.

"Now listen here," said the galoot. He didn't get to finish. Lana smashed the chair over his back, cheap wood breaking with a hollow *crack*. The shutterbugs went crazy, flashbulbs *fssh*ing and film *zzzip*ing as they snapped shot after shot of Lana's tantrum. "*Andale, andale,*" she screamed. "*La puerta.*" The words sent electricity through Flaco. He jumped, ran, almost made it to the door. One hard shove into the room's thin wall and a finger wagging tsk-tsk-tsk in his face was enough to make him reconsider. The thug grabbed Lana by the hair and smacked her face, front and back of the hand.

She didn't yelp but purple freckles of broken blood vessels scattered over her red cheeks all the same. He grabbed Flaco too, for good measure, and gave him the same. He cried out. Lana didn't. The photogs froze. Can't sell pictures of that.

"Jesus, Giuli," said Darkroom Louie. "She's expecting."

"She's expecting another smack if she don't change her tune. Now listen here," said the thug, lifting a fistful of Ron's hair and forcing him to look him in the eye. He kept talking, some tough guy falderol borrowed from penny dreadfuls and Monogram double features. Ron didn't listen. He caught his breath and looked across the room at Lana. Did she really just break a chair over this garlicky Bowery Boy wannabe? *Attagirl.*

Suddenly the photographers shielding their sunken chests with their heavy black garlands of camera equipment looked like eunuchs compared to his atomic-powered hellcat of a wife. His mouth twisted up in a smile.

"Excuse me." Ron caught a swat on the cheek. "Something funny?"

"I was just thinking," said Ron. "Why are you here?"

"You don't listen too good, do you, Ronnie? I gotta tell you again?"

"No, that I understand. Rockwell's feelings are hurt. You need to make a buck. And we're sickos anyway. If this was billiards, it'd be a perfect three-shot. With an eightball in the corner pocket to win the game." He turned to the photographers. "Did you get what you needed?"

The photographers looked at each other. Ron watched the thought percolate between their ears. *Shit, no, we didn't. We busted down the door because we got such a thrill being in Giuli the Battering Ram's wrecking crew, and all we've got to show for it is pics of Lana busting chairs over someone who doesn't want his face in the papers. We needed kissing pics. Sicko pics. Nauseating mincing fag party pics. We got zip. Bupkus. Nada nada limonada.* He could almost see the winged dollar bills flapping away from their pockets.

"Can I oblige you?" said Ron.

"Can you *oblige* me?" said Giuli, feigning outrage as he wracked his inadequate vocabulary.

"Not you. Your work is done. Them." He nodded his head to the photographers. "I mean, you came all the way here to prove that Ron Dash is a true-baby-blue fag. And I am. I've grown quite fond of trim on occasion, thanks to the lovely woman here that you've treated so *very* poorly," he said, real outrage coloring his speech. "But it's true. You've got me. There's nothing quite so sweet in this world as the inside of a boy's ass wrapped around your hard cock. Or vicey versa." The men holding him dropped his arms in reflex revulsion, just as Ron figured they would. He straightened up, combed his fingers through his hair, strode to Giuli and stared calmly into his squinting, flinching eyes. "The only thing that comes close is the slide of a boy's foreskin under your tongue. A boy trussed to a bed, that is, naked and willing to be burned with cigarettes."

"Why, you sick little—"

"Uh-uh, Giuli." Darkroom Louie stepped in. "You break it, you buy it."

He raised his camera. "Smile for the birdie, champ?"

"Sure," smiled Ron, and strode over to where Flaco stood, naked and shivering.

"You like humiliation?"

"Yes." His stiffening cock chimed in assent.

"Your mother can never read your name in the papers again, you know."

"Neither can yours. I don't care." His eyes were glassy and shining with anticipation. "This is what I want."

Lana's face was twisted with worry. "Ron, what are you doing?" she whispered.

Ron walked to her. He took her forearms in his fists, yanked her close, hovered his face a delicious moment over hers. Then he kissed her, fiercely. Flashbulbs snapped. He didn't care.

"We can be free," he said.

Then he let her go.

"Hey, Snaps." Ron crooked his finger. Darkroom Louie stepped forward.

"You shot our wedding, right?"

"Happiest day in a girl's life. I hear Lana had a good time, too."

"You make good coin?"

Louie lifted the replacement Leica from around his neck. "I bought a new lens for my good camera. It was great until someone busted it. I think they still owe me."

"Maybe so. You know what sells better than weddings?" He walked back to Flaco. "Honeymoons."

He turned to Flaco and grabbed a fistful of his dark hair. He was going to do something, to another man, for a roomful of witnesses. Thirty-six years of shame reared up inside him. Thirty-six years of being the sissy kid and the odd duck and the queer. He looked into Flaco's crystalline blue eyes. Blue skies. The wild blue yonder. It gave him strength. He dredged up the trash of thirty-six years of self-hate. He dumped it into the incinerator inside him. He felt it burn down to ash. A strange choking weight suddenly lifted from his heart. His hands flew to Flaco's neck, to the soft space underneath his porcelain jaw, and pulled him close.

He kissed him. Flaco didn't fight him. He opened his yielding mouth without complaint and slid his tongue against Ron's. Giuli didn't stick around. The big man fled to the door as if man love was contagious. An elephant, scared of a mouse. The door slammed behind him. Ron looked at the photographers still assembled. They clutched their cameras and tucked their chins low so no one would see they weren't so hard-boiled. Only Darkroom Louie coolly snapped another roll of film into his camera.

"You boys forgot to take a picture," laughed Ron. "Take two?"

"Rewrite," said Lana. She stepped forward, topaz eyes rich with some private joke. "I want in on this scene."

"I'm sure you do. But you're overdressed."

"Talk to wardrobe." She shrugged the white blouse off her shoulders. Now the photographers perked up at attention, professional hopes of a hot saleable shot and private hopes to see a movie star in the all-together

221

merging for one hot moment. Lana felt the temperature in the room change. She shrugged her blouse back up over her shoulders and gave the men an eviscerating stare.

"Ok, fellas," she said. "You want to see a woman?"

She pulled down her skirt. The photographers blanched at the sight of the triangular shock of dull honey-colored hair coasting at the top of her thighs, right under the swell of her belly. It was not a way they were accustomed to seeing movie stars. It was not a way they were accustomed to seeing women, period.

"Are you afraid of me?" said Lana in a mocking baby voice. The men didn't answer, their silence speaking volumes.

"I'm not," said Ron. He reached to her and kissed her again. One hand swept over the swell of her belly, to the honey patch at the bottom. He cupped it gently as he lavished kisses over her neck. She reached up and unbuttoned her blouse. Her nipples were wide-ringed and deep brown now, full and ready for the baby still nestled in her belly. Ron looked at her with admiration.

"You're beautiful," he said. He turned to the photographers. "Fellas, don't you agree?"

The men nodded mutely, terrified. They were cowed and awed by this slip of a woman. Naked, in the dim light, she looked like a marble fertility goddess, and the men knew their puny cameras and piddling assignments were mere distractions compared to the vital task this mother-to-be had undertaken. They could not bring themselves to photograph her, just as men must not stare directly at an eclipse.

He gave Lana one last, courtly kiss on the back of her hand, and then sidled over to Flaco. There were no words between them. Their mouths cleaved together wordlessly and their kiss was deep and true. Ron's hands searched over Flaco's body, over the swerve of his narrow waist and the hard axe edge of his hipbones and the vital, twitching sinew felt through the thin skin of his back.

"I love you," he whispered again in Flaco's mouth.

The room and the bed and the crowd fell away. In this dreamless, fearless space there was only Flaco, the culmination of everything Ron had ever dreamed of. He flipped him onto the bed and drove his cock true into the boy's willing ass. The boy bucked and reared and grabbed at the sheets, his face contorted in salty-sweet pleasure, his mouth open and panting and whispering for more. Ron obliged, burying his cock in the tight warm space that grew warmer and tighter with each thrust. It was more exquisite because he knew now how it felt, to trust someone enough to allow them to do this. His own ass still burned with the pleasurable ache of how Flaco had done this to him. The symmetry of how they'd violated each other's bodies excited him. *We are the same,* he thought. Same pleasure, same trust, same deep abiding connection in the heart. He had never before fucked—no, made *love*—in this symmetrical, passionate way. It was sweeter and deeper and truer than anything he'd ever known. *I am in the same place as you, Flaco,* he thought, his heart swelling with gratitude. *And I never want to leave. When* he came it was not with the finality of the end. It was a beginning, and he cuddled close to Flaco and savored the glow.

Even though he couldn't see the photographers, he could hear the sounds perfectly. The soft sigh of disgust that announced this tableau was too rich for even these hard-boiled photographers' blood. The grunt of realization that these pics would never sell, to anybody, for any price. No magazine would run them. Blackmailers can't use guilty parties who refuse to feel guilty. The best they could do was print up a few glossies and share them with photographer buddies, the ones they could trust not to call the cops and tattle about their hot archive. In the space between sighs they calculated the cost of air fare to Miami and figured they'd better get some shots of beach beauties to justify the trip before their plane dumped them back in L.A. One by one they filed out the door, dispirited. Some even ripped their film out of their cameras and dumped it on the floor in sad grey curlicues. Not even a goodbye.

Darkroom Louie didn't split. He came in close, carefully, eyes shining with perception. Ron could feel him circling their bodies, hear the soft *znip* of the shutter, the voyeur's butterfly kisses. It didn't disturb him, to be seen like this, as he crested his lover's body, as his wife curled on her side against them and stroked their hair, nudged her back against their warm flesh, didn't shrug off Flaco's lazy, generous hand taking a moment to circle the soft flesh between her legs, her gentle kiss on his forehead, his return of his hand to Ron's body. Every photo was careful in a way Ron had never been photographed before. Careful, and respectful. Louie reeled up the film reverently and placed it on the table. "Here's your honeymoon pics," he said. Then he tipped his hat and slipped silently out the door.

"Wait," said Ron. He snatched the roll up off the table and placed it in Louie's palm. "Your retirement fund," he said. "Fifty years from now we'll all be Hollywood history six feet under at Forest Lawn. Write your tell-all then. I'll sleep good knowing my shipwrecked reputation helped a friend out in the end."

Louie looked carefully at the roll of film. He tossed it gently in his palm, as if weighing it, and shook his head. "Too hot to handle, pal." But he smiled and put it in his pocket. "Maybe that'll change. I'll take the chance. I always did had a knack for being the last man standing. So long, Dickie." He nodded at Lana, and then at Flaco. "The kid from Armonk finally got something right."

"I need one more favor, pal."

"I'm ahead of you. Come with me, little lady," he said to Lana. He scooped her blouse up off the floor and handed it to her. "We'll hightail it back to La-la land in style. I've got an Army buddy with his own Cessna. It's idling on the tarmac as we speak."

"I'll take you up on that," she said. She turned to Ron. "I'll do the paperwork when I get back," she said, buttoning her blouse.

"I'll take the fall. You can charge me with adultery. We'll stage a scene."

"It's not necessary." She wriggled into her skirt. "I'll go to Mexico for a few days. It's easier that way. Plus I get to see my boys at the racetrack again. I want to see how La Corderita's doing." She walked over to Ron and put her hand on his chest. "The jockeys think she'll—"

A sudden splatter of liquid soaked both of their toes, as if a water balloon had popped between Lana's legs.

"Oh my god," said Lana. An echoless silence struck the room like a blunt object at the back of the head. They locked eyes.

"Oh my god," she said, and meant it.

30

"Take the rental," said Louie, tossing Ron the keys to the Pontiac parked outside. Flaco snatched the keys out of the air. "I'll drive," he said. "You get in the back with her." They clambered inside, Ron and Lana in the back. Louie leaned in the window. "There's a hospital on 12th," he pointed. "Follow the signs. There's a map in the glove compartment if you get lost. I'll take a taxi back to the airfield." He rapped the roof twice and saluted them from the curb as they peeled out.

Ron held Lana's hand tightly as Flaco screeched around the corner. "Does it hurt?" he asked.

"No," she said. "Should it hurt? I don't know." She gripped his hand back just as fiercely and Ron saw a panic in her eyes that he'd never seen before.

"I don't see any signs," said Flaco. He flipped open the glove compartment and rooted around, one eye on the road he was tearing down. "Here." He tossed the map into the back seat.

"We can't go to the hospital," said Lana. "They're looking for us. Once Rockwell gets word of how we crossed him he'll send out the real goons."

"We've got to," said Ron. "We'll take that chance."

"I'm not in pain," said Lana. "We'll go to a hotel room. We'll wait it out. I can have the baby there."

"Don't be stupid. We've been over this."

"You are not my doctor and you are not me." The familiar fierce fire crackled up in her eyes. "I can do this," she snarled. "I *will* do this."

"You've got to do this, Lana," said Flaco. "*Considera el bebé.*"

Her plea broke into a wounded animal sob. "Don't make me go to a hospital," she wept. Her tiny body shook with a convulsive shudder. "Hospitals are where mothers go to die. I can't. I'm not brave. I'm not brave like you think I am. Oh, Mommy. Please. I'll have this baby anywhere but there. Please don't make me," she wailed into her chest. "Oh god, it hurts now. It hurts." She lay her hand on her belly and inhaled sharply. Ron noticed with horror that there were twin rivulets of blood snaking their way down her thighs to her ankles.

"Lana," said Ron, clutching her hand tightly, "I got you into this mess and so help me God, I'm going to get you and our baby out of it."

"But where?" Lana looked at him, tears streaked down her reddened cheeks, two snail tracks running in parallel with the blood rivers down her white thighs. "What are we going to do? There's nowhere in the world for us. Nowhere we can be safe. Not anymore."

She was right. Despair clouded Ron's thoughts for one ugly moment, but something glimmered through. A small spark of a memory from the morning—my god, had this months's worth of turmoil only taken place in the span of one day? The idea bursting loose in his brain felt like a divine visitation from another lifetime, but it was the answer. It was perfect and clean and if all the stars were aligned it would be exactly what they needed.

A wave of calm washed over him. He unfolded the map and as his eyes scanned for the target Flaco's whisper floated back to the backseat as if he could read Ron's thoughts: *Dios te salve, María, llena eres de gracia, el Señor es contigo.*

31

The vine-covered marble edifice at Hialeah Park was just as grand as the ad men promised it would be, but Lana was having none of it. She retched in his lap as Ron scanned the gates frantically as Flaco screeched around the turns. "Come on, come on . . ." he whispered urgently to himself. Where would they have parked the trailer? Would they have made the trip back to Tampa already? Or stayed the night? He could hear her whimpering softly. "Easy, Lana." He tried to make his voice as soft and comforting as a stallion's snort. "We're here. Smell the hay. Listen." The pealing chirps of pre-dawn crickets sang out in a sparkling choir. They caught a whiff of the musky turf smell of manure, perfume only to those who love the races. Lana looked up a moment, lip quivering and face green. Something in her melted momentarily before another pain seized her up and bent her double. "Horses," he whispered to her, stroking her hair. "There are horses here."

Joy swelled up in his heart when he spotted the long vitamin capsule of a trailer outside the stables. "Here. Here!" he shouted to Flaco. They jerked to a halt and Ron jumped out of the car. He pounded on the door, heart in his throat. A light switched on inside, illuminating a thin lozenge of a window. Ron allowed himself to exhale. The aluminum door creaked open and a befuddled and stout Cuban man stood there, blinking in his pajamas.

"Are you the horse doctor?" shouted Ron.

"Yes," said the baffled man. He rubbed his eyes.

"We need your help," he said. "She's having a baby."

He jolted at the words. "There's a phone in the stables. I'll call an ambulance."

"No. Please. It's an emergency. She's bleeding. We need your help." The man's eyes went wide and jaw dropped and Ron turned to see what had shocked him so. Lana was staggering out of the car by herself. Flaco jumped out of the driver's seat and raced around to support her like a wounded soldier an instant before her knees gave way. The insides of her legs were now thick with gore.

"*Por favor*," she said, eyes praying. "*Ayuadame*."

The sight of her jarred him into action. "*Conmoverla al interior.*" He swung the trailer door wide open. "*Ándale, ándale.*"

They went into the trailer. It was narrow but comfortable, with a breakfast nook and dresser drawers in the pine walls and yesterday's coffee in a tarnished espresso maker on the hot plate. A black alligator doctor's bag squatted on the stub of a kitchen table. A plain but new single bed clung close to the far wall. The doctor pulled bath towels from the drawers and lay them in a patchwork on the coverlet before laying her down gingerly.

"You're a veterinarian?" Lana panted.

"No," he said. He yanked open another drawer and removed a stethescope. "In Cuba I'm a doctor. Here I can only work on horses." He put the ends into his ears with quick efficiency and pressed the cold circle against her belly, brows furrowed in concentration. "She may have placenta previa." His thick hands palpated her belly. "The baby is not yet in distress. But we've got to get it out."

"What do you mean, get it out?"

"We've got to do a C-section. Get her out of her clothes." Ron hesitated. "Come on, my friend!" The doctor opened a cupboard over the hot plate and extracted a half-drank bottle of white rum. Lana gave a small strangled cry. She looked like she was going to vomit again. Ron leaned over her. "I will not leave you," he said. "I'm staying right here." Together they unbuttoned her blouse and slid her skirt down to her ankles. The doctor sloshed the rum on a washcloth and wiped it over Lana's belly in lavish strokes. He snapped open the doctor's bag and extracted a hypodermic needle that looked big enough to knit with.

"You can't be serious," said Ron.

He plunged the needle into the rubber lid of a medicine vial. "This anesthetic is okay for horses and people," he said, drawing up a dose and tapping out the bubbles. "I'm sorry about the needle." He swiped her arm with the alcohol rag and pinned her wrist to the bed under his knee. "Don't look. In a moment you will remember nothing."

The needle plunged in. Her entire body cramped in agony for one torturous second before her eyes went glassy. Ron bit his lip and watched as her face slackened. Her inhalations and exhalations slowed to an ephemeral breeze. She turned her head as slowly as a sleepwalker to look at Ron. Her topaz eyes shone with dazzled revelation. She picked up Ron's hand as if in a dream, regarding the fingers and palm with the curiosity of an infant discovering her own toes. Then she kissed it. "I knew it wasn't going to last the day I met you," she murmured. She pressed his hand to his cheek. "You were still my best husband." Her eyes closed and her words melted away into silence. "I forgive you . . ."

The doctor was laying rum-sloshed scalpels out onto a folded towel. Ron kissed Lana's forehead as quietly as he could and extricated himself from her limp hand. On quiet feet he stole out the door.

Flaco was leaning against the car, biting a cuticle and staring a thousand-yard stare. Ron gently lowered his raw hand from his mouth.

"I don't like blood," said Flaco.

"I know," said Ron. He squeezed his hand tightly.

There was no sound from the trailer except for the silverware clicking of medical instruments. Ron lit a cigarette. He thought about pacing but that's what all expectant fathers do in the movies, don't they? He didn't want to live out a cliché but the itch to stalk back and forth was so insistent his feet decided in favor of it.

"Do you still love her?" asked Flaco.

The question caught Ron off guard. He looked at the slender beauty leaning against the car. The scant light glowing from the trailer's narrow windows danced in slivers across the planes of his face, writing the story of his good looks in slim liquid commas illuminating chin and cheekbone and brow and shoulders. Ron could see the trace of the elevator boy, the naïve sylph who'd broken something molten and true free inside the ice cave of Ron's heart, the someone whose joyously subordinate devotion wrote another surprise of a line in Ron's dry and stagnant biography. The Hollywood machine could scuff up his outsides but never touch the tender gem underneath. He could tell how his casual pose barely disguised a vulnerable tension about the axe Ron might drop on his heart.

Ron dropped his cigarette and ground it beneath his toe. He stood before Flaco and took his hands and looked him in the eye.

"Do you remember back in that shack in the strawberry fields?" said Ron. "And the picture of me from the movie magazines that you pasted on the wall?"

Flaco nodded. "I looked at you every night." His eyes glittered with welling tears.

Ron took a deep breath. "I didn't even know who you were until a year ago," he said, enunciating every syllable with tender care, "but now I know that, for all these years, I was looking back at you, too."

The door creaked and both men dropped each other's hands. The doctor poked his head out. He hadn't seen. "Hey, where did you go? I need you," he said. "Both of you. I can't do this operation alone."

Flaco froze. Ron grabbed him by the forearms.

"Blood is life," he said.

Flaco nodded and swallowed hard. Both men went into the trailer.

The doctor had set up a makeshift scrim from a sheet hanging from the ceiling. The amber light from a desk lamp illuminated the back of the sheet like a shadow puppet stage. A starburst of butter knives radiated from one of the hot plate's burners, each tip glowing hot. "Don't look at what I'm doing behind here, either of you." he told Flaco. "Just stay on this side with her. You—" he pointed to Flaco. "Keep your hand on her chest. Make sure she's breathing." Flaco knelt down to where Lana's head was and took her hand.. "And you," said the doctor, pointing at Ron. He handed him the last clean towel. "Wait right there."

He picked up a scalpel. His shadow hunched down low. Lana moaned but didn't stir. Ron bit his lip. It was taking too long, it had to be. He thought about ducking behind the sheet to see what was going on but suddenly the whole mattress shook as the doctor tugged vigorously on Lana's body. He grunted. There was a squelch and a pop and silence. In a flurry of movement the doctor handed something blue-gray and wet and flailing into Ron's hands. It took him a moment to realize it was a baby. It wasn't crying. "Rub her," the doctor said. *Her?* thought Ron. *It has a sex. It will have a name.* The doctor ran to the hot plate with a gloved hand and picked up the first of the white-hot butter knives. There was a sizzle and the smell of charred barbeque rose up in the compact space. Ron rubbed the blue thing with a towel. He rubbed as fiercely as someone wishing on a magic lamp. The baby gave a wet choke and a gasp and finally a lusty wail. The blue tone faded from its skin as it blossomed to a healthy pink.

The sun was dawning outside. The black of night gave way to lavender morning, that magic hour when anything is possible.

"We have a daughter," said Ron. He was amazed and moved. "Thank you," he told the doctor.

"Never tell anyone what just happened," the doctor said.

"I promise," said Ron. He leaned in to where Lana was laying dazed, held the baby close to her face, let her smell him. Love spilled over him and washed away his shock. This little creature with its angry fists and squalling squashed face was a lifetime in his hands. He bundled her protectively in the towel and held her close.

"Now what?" he said to Lana, meaning how were they going to be parents now.

Even under the haze of anesthesia the smirk of old Lana came back. "We make some phone calls," said Lana. "And we run."

32

Los Angeles Herald Express
February 2, 1958

AGENT PINCHED IN PORN RING

AP—The office of longtime Hollywood agent Edgar Rockwell was raided today by federal agents on charges of distribution of obscene material, human trafficking, and contributing to the delinquency of a minor. Rockwell, who'd made his living professionally representing many Hollywood actors, had been secretly connected to other pornography traffickers. An unrelated raid in Los Cruces led law enforcement to the agent's home, where they discovered a stash of over 5,000 obscene photographs, as well as evidence Rockwell also ran a boys-for-hire scheme. Police are also investigating connections between the scandal magazine Do Tell and Rockwell's photo archive. Bail has not been set.

Miami Daily News
February 3, 1958

ACTRESS SOUGHT BY FBI

The FBI issued an all-points bulletin for the whereabouts of motion picture actress Lana Arleaux Dash, an avowed Communist whose last known whereabouts were in the Miami area on or about January 1958. The actress is wanted for questioning on suspicion of espionage and treason, as well as her connection to the recent arrest of Hollywood agent Edgar Rockwell. Arleaux, aka Victoria Anne-Marie Schultz, is married to Rockwell client Ron Dash, one of the men noted in the report as appearing in Rockwell's pornographic photos. The FBI urges citizens to keep a look out for both Mr. and Mrs. Dash, noting that Mrs. Dash is expecting and may require medical attention. The Dashes may also be traveling in the company of Pace Hammond, aka Flaco Sandoval, a resident alien whose O-1B visa has been revoked. The trio may be in hiding in Los Angeles, Baja California, or may have traveled together to Cuba.

33

Havana, 1958

Ron was drinking *cuba libres*, heavy on the *libre* with lots and lots of ice. The sun dipped coyly behind coconut palms, exuberant Cuban sunshine mellowing to an early evening glow. No one else was on the sandy hotel patio save the mahogany-skinned dishwasher dealing out unhurried hands of solitaire, waiting for buddies to show up for cold Hatueys and loud hands of *mentirosa*. Three brown-skinned kids darted and laughed further out on the white sugar beach. The tallest girl stood proud in a white cotton eyelet dress, the wind churning the ruffles into sea foam froth. Her blackberry-dark hair was thick as combed wool and her wide eyebrows framed her eyes in merry apostrophes. Ron watched her. He thought about fearless girls he knew, how bravely they stand in white cotton and how nothing ugly can truly touch them. The girl's feet were bare. Ron was inspired. He slid off his sandals and scrunched his toes in the sand.

The hotel concierge in a trim white jacket stepped up to Ron. A pale blue envelope rested on the silver tray in his hand. "Una carta, señor." Ron opened the envelope gently. There was a photo booth strip of portraits inside. A merry, dark-haired matron he'd never seen before, holding a red-cheeked, floss-haired baby. Photo one, the woman holding the baby up in her tan hands, fingers pressing into the pretty smocked pinafore. Photo two, nudging a smile out of the baby with kisses and gentle pinches. Photo three, no luck. Baby still staring solemnly at the lens. Picture four, success. The baby eyes twinkling, her mouth open in a big gummy grin. Something soared in Ron as he suddenly recognized the Lana-like light in the baby's eyes and the chubby cheeks of his own baby picture. *My girl.* Tears welled in his eyes. He was so entranced it took him a moment to notice the letter fallen into his lap.

Dear Poppa,

I got Dr. de la Cuesta's wife Malena to take little Corazón to a photo booth on Calle Ocho. Maybe I'm paranoid but I don't want any photos of the two of us together. I've been photographed enough by Hollywood's big eye and I don't wish that on our baby. It's not her fault she's got such notorious parents.

The Dr. and Mrs. are taking good care of me. I'm glad you weren't around to see it, and this is the first I'm telling you, but I needed another operation to fix the emergency, and as it shakes out I'm done having children. Don't worry, I'm in good hands. Dr. is a very good doctor and I'm glad the thank-you cash we gave him is helping him speed through the approval process to practice medicine in this country. My belly is a mess with criss-crossing football scars but I don't care. I'm not sure being beautiful ever helped me and I'm looking forward to being the opposite. I see open terrain in the land of the fearlessly scarred.

When I'm recovered enough I'll come join you and Flaco in Havana. I want you to see Corazón, how big and adorable she is, how her eyes light up, how her smiles are sincere. But we can't stay long, because Cora and I will go on to Mayabeque, to the collective farm and orphanage I've been giving money to for years. It's the only place for us now that the State Department is breathing down my neck, and when I get there all I'll have to give is manual labor instead of Yanqui dollars, but they've assured me there's a place for us. Cora's siblings will be the other children of the revolution.

Which brings me to my next point—you and Flaco, keep your noses clean in Havana. It might be a worker's paradise but they've got homosexuality mixed up with all sorts of other capitalist decadence, and there's no changing anyone's mind. So as far as anyone's concerned, you're a rich American and Flaco's your loyal manservant—got it? I and other party members are looking to change that. We can do it from the inside. We're quick and we're smart and we'll land on our feet, no matter where we go. Besides, like Emma Goldman said, "If I can't dance, I don't want to be part of your revolution."

I never imagined this is where we would be today, that first afternoon you met me for drinks at DeLang's. I was a fright that day, two weeks in on a three week binge. Sadder than I'd ever admit to anyone, including myself. I've the knack for getting witty when hurt badly. It's how I've always survived. Did you know I never threw out that napkin on which I drew that lipstick heart? I kept it in my purse all these years. I don't know why. But yesterday I did. I opened the window and let it flutter out on the breeze. It was your heart, and I was keeping it safe until it went to the one it belonged to. And you gave me la corazón. *So we're square.*

Love to you and your hubby,

Viva la revolución,

L.

Ron folded the letter and tucked it in his jacket pocket. He folded the photo strip in careful fourths, stopping to marvel for one moment more at Cora's big smile. She looks so happy, he thought, and then, with a sudden flash of revelation, realized that he was happy, too.

The sun was going down. A slim figure surfaced from the waves. He was young and tan and shirtless and barefoot, a Mexico-by-California transplant effortlessly gone native once more. He carried a speargun over his shoulder and dangled a string of still-gasping parrotfish in his hand like fat lapis beads on a string. His dark hair hung in wet, unBrylcreemed curls over his forehead, and against the cool cerulean sky Ron admired the nosebreak hiccup in his once too-perfect profile.

In a few moments Flaco would hand the fish over to the kitchen man, chat in Spanish about this herb and that splash of lime—Ron was getting good at understanding their banter, he could now hear meaning in what was merely music before—and go clean up in their hotel room. Ron would follow Flaco to the room, catch him in the shower, slide soap over his smooth chest and stroke the hardening skin of his cock in the wet spray, kiss him fiercely, and then surrender, let Flaco have his way with him, let Flaco wrestle him and suck him and penetrate him with conscious, ecstatic abandon. And the two of them, bodies intertwined, would talk and nuzzle and tease each other's nipples, and then duck into the shower again, dress for dinner, eat parrotfish beautifully grilled with just a hint of lime, and drink sugarcane sangria into the wee hours until no one cared that two men slowly, tenderly paced the dance floor, arms wrapped around each other, eyes closed and deeply at peace.

All this was coming in a bright and limitless future. He saw it now, one moment after another flipping out like the dishwasher dealing cards from the top of the deck. Finally, it was good to be the king of his own destiny, one-eyed jack and his perfect crooked profile beside him, and the queen who changed his life. Why no princess in a deck of cards? Isn't there room for Cora, *princesa de corazónes*, and all the love overflowing towards her from her unconventional parents' hearts? Didn't matter. Ron knew his future wasn't bound to the worn-edged deck the dishwasher shuffled.

His future was his own, every shining moment of it. *I'll make things good for Cora*, he thought. *She'll never live a day in her life wishing she was someone—or something—else. That's my promise, to everyone I love.* He tapped himself on the chest, gently, with new and true affection. *Present company included.*

"Hey." Flaco's hand on his shoulder brought Ron out of his reveries. "Lost in dreams?"

"Not anymore," said Ron. He reached up to Flaco, gently lowered his face to his. *Flaco, mi amor.* Brown eyes shining. *Esperanza.* At last, one perfect kiss.

For Mom and Dad,
the real Hollywood happy ending.

VIOLET LEVOIT is a film critic and novelist. A former Emmy-winning PBS producer, Violet began her writing career as a film critic and arts journalist for Baltimore City Paper. Her work appears at Turner Classic Movies, Allmovie, PressPlay, Bright Lights Film Journal, Film Threat, and others. She is a contributor to the film history compendium *Little Black Book: Movies* (Cassell Illustrated). She is the author of five books, including the critically-acclaimed dark Hollywood tale *I Miss the World* (King Shot Press). She is also Associate Editor and Researcher for the Eisner-award-winning graphic novel publisher Beehive Books. Originally from Baltimore, she lives in Philadelphia.

Available from King Shot Press

Leverage by Eric Nelson
Strategies Against Nature by Cody Goodfellow
Killer &Victim by Chris Lambert
Marigold by Troy James Weaver
Noctuidae by Scott Nicolay
I Miss The World by Violet LeVoit
All-Monster Action by Cody Goodfellow
Nasty (ed. Tiffany Scandal)
Drift by Chris Campanioni
The Deadheart Shelters by Forrest Armstrong
The Yeezus Book
Blood and Water by J David Osborne
Scarstruck by Violet LeVoit

CPSIA information can be obtained
at www.ICGtesting.com
Printed in the USA
LVHW091739251019
635356LV00002B/381/P